IGNITED

THE IMMORTAL ONES - BOOK FOUR

Shade Owens

SERIES INFORMATION

Chosen - Book One
Evolved – Book Two
Hunted – Book Three
Ignited – Book Four
Risen – Book Five

Edited by Nikki Busch
www.nikkibuschediting.com

Published by

RED RAVEN PUBLISHING

ISBN: 978-1-990775-17-8

CHAPTER 1

I felt the snap of my crossbow's string but couldn't hear it with all the chaos around me.

Up ahead, my bolt penetrated the shoulder of a lean, female Woodface. Although I couldn't see her face behind her tribal wooden mask, she must have cried out in pain; she threw her head back, the mask sliding up a few inches above her chin, and grabbed the bolt stuck in her shoulder.

Her head snapped toward me, her dark, angry eyes floating behind two circles carved in the mask.

It was a dreadful stare that made me wish I'd killed her instantly.

Around me, people screamed and ran in all directions. Bodies bumped into me as swords, sticks, and batons swung through the air. The sound of bones snapping sent chills up my spine. With all the screaming, stomping, and clashing of weapons, I wasn't so sure I'd heard it right. So I looked twice, only to spot a man with his mouth agape as he reached for his deformed leg.

I scanned my surroundings, my vision pulsating.

There had to be another weapon here.

Something better than my crossbow. Although it had initially served its purpose, the Woodfaces had pushed too far into the courtyard, and we were dealing with close-range combat. With everyone crammed so close, it was impossible to land a clear shot.

Yet before I could find a useful weapon lying on the ground, something fast-moving caught my eye—something running toward me. I raised my head in time to spot the woman I'd shot sprinting toward me, a wild look on her face. She ran screaming with her mouth wide open, though I couldn't hear her, and in her right hand was my crossbow's bloody bolt—the same one I'd used to shoot her.

I stiffened, preparing myself to knock her across the face with my entire crossbow, when a long baton swung down near her shins.

Clack.

Ungracefully, something or someone propelled her forward before she landed flat on her face.

Who struck her?

There were too many people around me.

I expected her to rise, but she didn't have the time.

Within seconds, three of her people trampled her as they tried to dodge our attack.

They hadn't seen her under them, but I had.

I watched, mortified, as their large feet forced her face into the dirt, crushed her chest, and broke her arms.

When her mask fell off, her brown eyes were squinted in pain. Her hair, now clumps of brown, stuck to her grimy forehead, her neck, and her shoulders. She had a short face, though it elongated as she cried out, her mouth wide open.

With her uncrushed arm, she reached out and mouthed something.

I couldn't tell if she was asking for help or asking them to get off of her. Tears streamed from the corners of her eyes as she pleaded silently, praying for the pain to stop.

But no one noticed her.

No one but me.

With trembling hands, I loaded another bolt, preparing to shoot her in the head. Although the last thing I wanted was to fire a bolt through someone's eye—the thought made me sick to my stomach—it was better than watching her slowly die of a collapsed chest.

I clicked my bolt into place, but before I could even raise my crossbow, a dead body fell on top of her, and the crowd grew thicker and thicker, until she disappeared entirely.

Suddenly, something came at me in my peripheral.

I couldn't tell what it was—but I sensed it coming straight for my head.

I ducked in time, feeling a spiked wooden club graze the top of my head, then angrily smashed my crossbow into the Woodface's ribs.

He bent forward, clutching his injured abdomen.

I stared at his club.

Then, I did something stupid; I lunged at him, trying to pry the weapon from his hands.

But he was too strong. Even with a single-handed grip and a fresh abdominal injury, he held on to it. It was like trying to pull a door off its hinges and made me feel weak and helpless.

Maybe hand-to-hand combat wasn't for me.

Immediately, I let go of the club and picked my crossbow from the grass. With trembling legs, I ran away from the battle's density.

I had to get out. I needed distance if I wanted to contribute to this fight.

As more and more people shouted and blood splattered throughout Fort Denton's courtyard, I wondered if maybe this was all nothing but a nightmare.

A dream. A horrible dream.

For all I knew, this wasn't even real.

Maybe all the chaos and bloodshed I'd seen

over the last few months had caused me to have highly vivid nightmares.

Warm blood suddenly splattered across my chin, coating my lips with an iron taste. I watched, eyes wide, as a young man in front of me reached for his throat and gargled, trying to stop the fountain of blood from spilling out. Next to him stood a Woodface twice my size, with massive shoulders that almost looked nonhuman. He held a long rust-colored sword in one hand and smashed his chest with his other fist. The impact against his body caused his countless black braids to hop off his shoulders on either side of his bloodstained mask.

When dark eyes rolled toward me, I knew I was next.

I raised my crossbow, no longer remembering if I'd even loaded it, but it was no use.

Without warning, someone accidentally crashed into me, and my crossbow flew out of my hands as if it weighed nothing more than a river stone.

Although I couldn't see the large Woodface's features, I got the feeling he was smiling at me.

Now that I was weaponless, he'd get to enjoy his kill.

With a loud grunt, he raised his sword, preparing to slash it straight through my neck.

Out of nowhere, something loud caught everyone off guard. Several people flinched, and others dropped to the ground instantly.

Even the Woodface froze for a moment, trying to understand what was happening.

Then the sound went off again.

Bang. Bang. Bang.

I flinched and covered my ears.

While most Woodfaces were now in a panic, running around mindlessly, this big one wasn't prepared to let go of his kill. He repositioned his sword, tightened his shoulder muscles, and then...

Bang.

He jolted upright, dropped his sword, and stood still for a moment with both arms in the air. I couldn't tell if he was in shock, confused, or if his muscles had all contracted.

The bullet hole appeared right in the center of his chest.

Slowly, he reached for it, the tips of his fingers soaking up bright red blood.

Before he could even look up to see who had shot him, he fell to his knees, his armor shaking with the impact, and collapsed to his side, lifeless.

Without thinking, I threw myself into the grass, crawled over to his sword, and gripped it tightly. Staying down, I searched the battleground, trying to understand what was happening.

That's when I realized the only people being shot at were Woodfaces.

Closer to Fort Denton's entrance stood Sofia and Elias holding pistols. With arms straight in front of them, they fired shot after shot after shot, taking down our enemies.

Then, more of Elias's people drew their guns.

And these, unlike Elias's and Sofia's handheld guns, were much larger.

Rifles, I knew.

I stayed on the ground, covering my ears as the rifles went off, the loud *rat-a-tat-tat* sound making my hands vibrate over my ears.

Our people seemed to realize what was going on. More and more of us dropped to the ground, exposing the Woodfaces to the deadly bullets.

As much as I hated how loud the gunshots were, we needed them if we wanted to defeat these Woodfaces. Ahead, our enemies shook violently in the air as blood sprayed everywhere, landing on masks, faces, and weapons, even settling on the grass like morning dew. Many stumbled back before falling, while some collapsed instantly, piling over top of the other dead bodies.

I stared wide-eyed at the massacre, disturbed that such small pieces of metal could take lives so quickly. But it needed to be done. It was either them or us, and they were the ones who had attacked us first.

Within minutes, the bullets stopped, and white smoke floated around the shooters. Slowly, I removed my hands from my ears, as did the others inside the courtyard, and stood.

One by one, everyone else did the same. Some grabbed their weapons, and others left them on the ground next to dead bodies.

"Everyone okay?" Elias shouted, lowering his handgun.

His voice came out deep and resonated across the entire courtyard. I understood why he was the leader of this place. Or at least, used to be, before his brother Jared locked us out. I shifted my gaze to the iron door at the back of the courtyard—the one that led into the bunker. In the middle of it was a narrow gap wide enough for someone to look through.

My stomach knotted at the sight of Jared's dark, hateful slits floating on the other side of the opening. Although I couldn't see the rest of his face, I could tell he wasn't happy that we'd defeated the Woodfaces—wrinkles formed between his narrowing eyes.

He was angry. And why wouldn't he be?

He'd set this whole thing up, hoping we would all die for having chosen Elias over him.

I wanted to shout at him—accuse him of being a coward for using someone else's army to do his dirty work, but I didn't have the time. Without warning, a loud clicking sound came from behind the door, and slowly, it opened, revealing a lanky Jared carrying a gun three times the size of everyone else's.

CHAPTER 2

I tightened my grip around my crossbow and quickly loaded another bolt.

All I wanted was to fire it straight into Jared's throat. How could he have done this? How could he have sacrificed all these people? I spun in circles, taking in the scene around me.

While many of us were armed with weapons, many were not. Most of the people who had lived here before we arrived were ordinary people—they weren't fighters. They tended to gardens and collected eggs from the chicken coop every morning. These people hadn't deserved to see such violence.

One family in particular—two teenage girls and their parents—huddled in a tight group at the far back of the courtyard, away from the bloody scene. Their faces were covered with dirt, and their clothes looked like they were several decades old. The four of them trembled together. The mother tried to cover her girls' eyes with her hands, but the young teenagers simply pried her fingers away and swayed their heads sideways, not wanting to miss anything.

These were innocent people.

The farther I searched the open courtyard, the more children I found. Most of them lay next to the garden beds with their faces snuggled in the ground. A few adults stood nearby, snapping their fingers and pointing downward every time a child's head popped up.

It made me sick to my stomach.

It also reminded me of Lutum and the life I swore I'd never go back to.

Jared stepped out of the bunker, his bristly chin aimed so high that his Adam's apple came into view.

At once, Elias raised his gun, as did every other gun-carrying fighter behind him.

"There won't be any need for that," Jared said.

He smiled, and I slowly raised my crossbow. But before I could gaze down its sight, my bow was forcibly lowered by something heavy.

Next to me, Sadie used her baton to lower my crossbow. "Don't do it."

I sighed.

She was right.

If I tried anything, I risked the lives of everyone inside the courtyard.

Elias had this covered, and I had to trust he knew how to manage his brother.

"Lower your weapons," Jared shouted.

Through the dark opening behind him came dozens more of his men armed from head to toe. They wore black helmets with shiny glass that reminded me of Lutum's Defenders. My heart thudded hard as I was pulled back into my past, but Sadie's warm touch snapped me back to reality.

"You okay?" she whispered.

Had my heart been beating *that* loudly?

"You look tense," she added.

I realized I'd been digging my nails into the metal of my crossbow's handle.

"I'm okay," I lied.

"Lower your weapons!" Jared shouted again.

He stepped forward, his tall, lanky figure looking too weak to carry the massive gun in his grasp. Without hesitating, he propped it up and pointed it at Elias.

But Elias didn't drop his gun as ordered. Instead, he stood with his shoulders drawn back, staring at his brother without blinking. "Not a chance," he said.

On our side, men and women did the same as Elias—they kept their rifles raised at Jared and the other traitors. I glared at the people standing behind Jared. Why were they even following him? Elias had been in charge of the bunker. Why turn on him? As far as I could tell, Elias was a much better leader than his brother.

Then, I thought back to when he first allowed us inside the bunker. Many of his people had been enraged with his decision, saying that we would only cause famine and take from their resources.

With his gun pointed at Jared, Elias elevated his chin. "What do you want? You already have the bunker."

Jared tilted his head and smiled playfully. He then dropped his gun to his side like he didn't even care about it and said, "You're right, brother. I got what I wanted. The bunker. But as you very well know, this place won't maintain itself. I need a few volunteers—" He raised his gun again and started pointing it at people inside the courtyard.

Several screams erupted around us as people dove to the ground. Others stood still but raised their arms into the air. I wasn't sure what this gesture meant, but it appeared to represent submission of some kind.

"I want half," Jared said.

"Half?" Elias repeated. "Half of what?"

"Everything," Jared said, smirking like the monster he was.

It didn't make sense to me. These two men were brothers, yet Jared was acting like they were enemies. Did he resent Elias *that* much?

"You're insane," Elias blurted. "We aren't giving you half—"

Jared's brows came close together above his long nose. "I said half."

Stabilizing his gun with both hands, he pointed it at Elias once more.

Elias's back muscles tightened underneath his shirt. Even from back here, I could sense his anger. He was caught in a difficult position. How could he argue against someone pointing a gun at him? Not only that, but Jared had more gun-carrying fighters on his side. We only had about a dozen.

"Leave half of everything and get lost," Jared said.

"Fine," Elias said. He turned around, twirled a finger in the air, and shouted, "Take half of everything and get out."

Some of our fighters, also known as Champions, started clearing a path through the gates by dragging dead Woodfaces out of the way.

"Grab whatever you can," someone whispered, and people started prying weapons from cold fingers.

"Ah, ah, ah," Jared shouted.

At first, I thought maybe he'd spotted us taking weapons from the Woodfaces. But that wasn't the issue at all. He pointed at the far back of the courtyard, where innocent people had started migrating toward the gates.

"Half means people, too," Jared said.

"Have you lost your mind?" Elias growled.

"These people want nothing to do with you!"

Jared smirked evilly. "No? Let them decide for themselves."

Narrowing his hateful gaze, he stood quietly, then said, "Those of you who want safety and shelter, move to this side of the courtyard."

To my surprise, several people did precisely that. I blinked hard, trying to understand what was happening. Why were they joining Jared after he'd betrayed them?

"What are they—" I started, but Sadie cut me off.

"They're human," she said as if having experienced this before. "Humans get scared. Humans also have survival instincts, and right now, those people feel like their odds of survival are better here than out there, in the unknown."

"Exactly," Dax said, standing tall next to Sadie. "People are scared of change."

Blood spatter covered her sculpted jaw, but she didn't seem to notice. Aside from the speckles of red, she didn't appear injured. That woman was tougher than anyone I knew, and I was confident she'd handled herself just fine during the battle.

Sadie tied her wet, bloody hair into a bun at the back of her head. "At least they're choosing voluntarily."

Within minutes, dozens upon dozens of

people crossed the garden beds and joined Jared on the other side. I felt betrayed but reminded myself of Sadie's words. They were human. As in Lutum, these people were doing what they thought was their best chance at survival.

A few people cried and pleaded as family members chose the opposite side. One man tugged on a young girl's arm, while a woman did the same on the opposite side of the girl, trying to pull her toward the bunker.

People screamed, and others cried. In the end, many with children chose to stay behind.

"I want my son!" someone suddenly shouted.

Out from the crowd came a tall, dark-skinned man. He ran through the gardens and over children, his heavy feet stomping in the dirt.

He was headed straight for Jared.

"He's inside. Let him out!" the man shouted.

His voice was deep and projected across the entire courtyard. It was a loud, authoritative voice that seemed to irritate Jared.

Still, Jared didn't bother raising his gun.

He didn't have to.

At once, his soldiers raised their guns on the man marching his way over to Jared.

"Westin's dad," I mumbled.

"What?" Sadie asked.

I turned my head sideways to spot James looking back at me with huge eyes. He knew the truth, as did I. Westin wasn't inside the bunker. We'd told his father that he'd been injured and was receiving treatment in the medical unit. The injury part was factual—Jared had shot him through the leg inside a country home he also burned to the ground—but Westin wasn't here, in Fort Denton. We'd left him back in Lockridge—a lakeside village—so that he could receive proper medical care for his leg.

We were lucky to have been allowed entry into the village, but our welcome was thanks to Logan and his family—the people we'd saved from the burning home.

Still, I'd promised Ari, leader of Lockridge, that we wouldn't tell anyone about their secret village. So instead, we'd lied to Westin's father, hoping we'd somehow manage to return to Lockridge and bring Westin safely home.

His father knew none of this.

"Let him out!" he shouted.

Elias lunged sideways, stopping the large man in his tracks. "Easy, easy," he tried, but Westin's father threw him aside, and Elias fell to the ground as if weighing nothing more than a pine cone.

Several people gasped at the sight of their leader being tossed aside, but all I saw was a father terrified of never seeing his son again.

Without thinking, I dropped my crossbow and ran toward him. Several eyes darted my way, and I knew that I was about to put myself in a dangerous situation.

After everything that had happened with Jared, I suspected he wanted me dead.

So if he had any excuse to put a bullet through my head, he'd use it.

But I couldn't stand by and let Westin's father get himself killed.

"Stop!" I shouted.

My feet smacked hard against the dry soil as I ran toward Westin's father. He couldn't hear me, though, and was angry now—probably because Jared wasn't cooperating and instead stood quietly as his people aimed their guns straight ahead.

Veins bulged from the large man's neck as his movements quickened. Now, he was charging toward the bunker.

"My son!" he shouted.

He was a tall man with long legs, and no matter how hard I ran, I knew I wouldn't make it in time.

And right when I thought it was all over—when I prepared myself for bullets to fly into Westin's father—he did the unthinkable. Rather than blast past Jared and try to storm inside the bunker, he collapsed onto his knees, bowed his head, and pleaded with Jared.

"P-p-p-please, my son," he said. "He's

inside. Please let him out."

Jared smirked, probably enjoying being begged.

"You mean to tell me that you want me to go back into the bunker and get your son so that the two of you can walk out of here with"— he flicked a finger at Elias—"that man. With them."

That man, I thought.

His own brother, and he spoke of him as if he were nothing more than a stranger—a nuisance.

Jared made a sour face at the sight of his brother.

By the time I caught up with Westin's father, I stopped and stood quietly. The way he'd been charging full force, I had assumed he might try to harm Jared and get himself killed.

But he was begging.

Pleading for his son.

"P-p-please," he said again.

Jared elevated his chin. "You can either stay here with us, or you can leave with *them*."

No! I wanted to shout at Westin's father. *Westin is safe in Lockridge. He isn't here.*

The crying man turned his head slowly, his watery eyes aimed at Elias. It was like he was apologizing for what he was about to do.

"Then... I'll stay," he said.

"No!" I shouted, immediately realizing the mistake I'd made.

Jared's dark eyes shot up at me.

"Silver," he said, my name sounding like poison on the tip of his tongue.

Behind him, countless guns turned on me.

"Is there something you'd like to say?" Jared asked.

I swallowed hard. What was I supposed to do? I couldn't tell Westin's father the truth without revealing Lockridge, and I'd made a promise to keep that information a secret. More importantly, I couldn't give that information to Jared. He and his men would raid the place and probably kill all the people who lived there.

"You don't have to do this," I told Westin's father.

He watched me with great sadness, and I felt awful. I wanted to tell him everything—say to him that if he came with us, he'd see his son again. If he stayed here, he'd lose his son.

"I do," he said. "It's my son."

My throat tightened as I thought of Westin and how he'd react when he found out we had left his dad behind.

"Something on your mind?" Jared asked me.

He was testing me. It was like he knew that I knew something.

"No," I mumbled.

A warm hand suddenly reached for my shoulder, and I swung around, prepared to throw a punch, yet spotted Dax's rigid features.

"Whoa, easy," she said. She tilted her head sideways; a gesture meant to signify, *Follow me*, and guided me away from Jared and Westin's father. "There's nothing you can do."

I walked away, feeling defeated. In a sense, I felt like I'd let Westin down.

Sadie joined us, and then James appeared by my side.

He wore his bright red sunglasses on top of his head today, his pale, orange-yellow eyes staring into me. It was like he was trying to communicate something but knew he couldn't say it out loud.

He didn't have to.

I knew exactly what he was telling me.

We'll reunite them somehow.

James had been with me in Lockridge. He knew the truth.

I stared at his countless freckles, trying to imagine such a future. Would it be possible? Would we manage to get Westin's father back? I wasn't convinced.

I looked up to spot the rest of the crew that had been with me when we found Lockridge.

Adu.

Colton.

Sierra.

And Emma.

The four of them gave me the same look. And although Sadie and Dax wouldn't understand what it meant, I did. Without

words, they were telling me not to give up—
that the battle was far from over.

As we started exiting through the giant
courtyard doors, Jared called out.

"Half the livestock, too!"

Elias gritted his teeth, his jaw muscles
popping out. Without arguing, he nodded at
everyone as a way of saying, *Only half.*

Reina walked alongside Finn, and Maz
followed close behind, waving her scarred
arms in the air as she called out to her dogs. A
few Champions unleashed them from the
stables, and they ran toward her, their long
pink tongues dangling on the sides of their
frightening, sharp-toothed jaws.

"And Elias," Jared shouted over all the
whispers. "Clean up your mess."

He threw his chin out at all the dead
Woodfaces piled atop one another.

Elias stiffened and clenched a fist. "Sorry,
brother, but this is *your* mess. You caused this."

Jared frowned but didn't argue.

Slowly, we exited the courtyard, with our
fighters armed with guns at the very back of
the crowd. They walked backward with their
weapons raised, prepared to fire deadly blasts
at Jared and his soldiers.

Everyone remained quiet as we left. Almost
too quiet.

And it wasn't until the gates closed behind
us that some people collapsed to their knees

and sobbed. Others, like me, stood in disbelief, wondering how all this had happened so suddenly.

An unspoken question seemed to loom over all of us as curious eyes shot back and forth.

What were we going to do now?

CHAPTER 3

The bickering started as a loud whisper, almost like the sound people made when they'd awake in Lutum. They would often exit their homes, and whisper-quiet voices would fill the sky as they began talking about the dreams they'd had.

Grandma once told me to be careful when discussing my dreams because dreams led people to have *wild ideas*, whatever that meant. So the morning whispers never lasted long, and the moment everyone approached their working posts, they fell silent.

But today, silence didn't come.

Instead, the talking became louder and louder, making me want to cover my ears.

"Where are we going?"

"I have children! Elias! What are we going to do?"

The last woman to speak pulled her two toddlers against her hips, her palms squishing their cheeks against her abdomen until they turned pink.

"We have to go back!" one man shouted.

Someone next to him—a middle-aged man with a scruffy gray beard—cleared his throat and, with a roar, shouted, "They can't get away with this!"

I was surprised to see Finn standing so quietly next to Elias.

Why wasn't he saying anything? Maybe he didn't feel it was his place. When he caught me watching him, his lip twitched, like he was trying to smile but couldn't find the strength.

My lips did the same thing.

"What are we going to do?" someone else shouted, her words aimed at Elias.

Rather than comfort his people, he shifted his gaze toward the sky. He paused, inhaled a deep breath, then held it. When he finally let the air out of his lungs, I expected him to have a speech prepared, but he didn't. It was like he was frozen.

Reina's dark eyes shifted from Elias to Finn. Although she wasn't anyone's leader, she'd served as Finn's General since I'd met her, and everyone respected her. Today, however, she wasn't wearing her usual fighting gear like many other Champions around me. She must have had the day off, not expecting it to turn out this way.

"Everyone!" she shouted.

Her Champions stiffened their backs,

prepared to receive orders. A few horses neighed in the background, and birds flew off forest tree branches all around us.

Elias's gun-wielding people, however, didn't seem to know who she was or why she was speaking. They still listened out of respect.

"We need to move, now!" she said.

The bickering started again.

This time, Finn shouted, "Reina is right! We've just made enemies behind these walls. Standing here makes us targets."

"But where are we going?" someone asked.

A little blond girl looked up at Finn with big watery blue eyes. She watched him with a pout as if he held all the answers.

But he didn't. Even I knew that.

He smiled down at her, trying to reassure her.

Like Elias, his eyes seemed to glaze over. It was a look Grandma used to get when she got lost in thought. When I questioned her about it, she said she'd been thinking about the past. And by past, I knew she was referring to Grandpa William, who had died decades before. She rarely spoke of him, but she'd told me enough to know he'd been the love of her life or, as she often said, the only light in all of Lutum.

But Finn wasn't thinking about the past. His eyes grew wide, and his head shot up. "We're returning to Ortus."

An uproar spread through the crowd. Half the people looked confused, many having only briefly heard about Ortus through stories shared inside the bunker. Those from Ortus, however, seemed upset at the thought of returning to a village that the Woodfaces had attacked.

What was Finn thinking, anyway?

How could we return to a village full of burned-out homes? A village of ash and decay?

Finn's lips stretched into a grin, and he turned to Reina. "Think about it. The barn was still intact when we left. So was the hospital. We're surrounded by mountains that protect us. He threw a hand toward the courtyard's partially open gates, where countless bodies lay. "And now, the Woodfaces are gone."

"What about the Eye?" Reina whispered next to Finn.

The Eye, I remembered.

I thought back to that white *drone*, as Sadie had called it. It had been looking for me. Sure, Sadie had destroyed it, but what if more of those... *things*... came?

"What choice do we have?" Finn whispered back. "We have too many people and nowhere to go. The river has plenty of fish. It's the only way."

Someone suddenly screamed, and people scattered away from one of the bodies. Next to it stood a Champion with a spear stabbed into a Woodface's chest. He tore the spearhead out, its bloody tip dripping over our enemy's cracked wooden chest plate.

"What?" he said, shrugging. "He moved... He was still alive."

This only made people panic more.

"We don't have time for this," Finn said to Elias. "The longer we stand here talking about where we're going, the more at risk we become."

Elias nodded and puffed out his chest. It was like his leadership had somehow returned to his body.

"Finn is right," Elias said.

People calmed down and slowly moved away from the courtyard's gates.

"We need to take action now," he continued. "And if Finn believes his old village is our safest bet, then I say we listen to him."

Some people looked worried, others confused.

"You are all free to choose," Elias added. "I, for one, will follow Finn back to his village. I hope you will all do the same."

To my surprise, no one argued. At least not with Elias or Finn. A few people bickered among themselves, likely friends or family members having opposing views.

"I don't want to go," someone whispered near me. "How can we trust this Finn guy?"

"We have to," someone whispered back.

The whispering faded as the crowd moved. The group pressed on, leaving me no choice but to walk along with everyone else.

Slowly, we made our way out of the forest and back into the same field we'd almost died in—the one where the tornado came through.

I glanced back at the hundreds of people forming a thick line behind us.

Some rode on horses, but not many. We only had two carts with barely any food on them. It wasn't like we'd had time to pack anything. Not with Jared pointing his guns at us. Thankfully, the forest path was large enough to fit the carts, and those who couldn't walk—the injured and the elderly—sat on the wheeled structures.

I thought back to Jared and how he'd cast his own brother out of the bunker, Fort Denton. According to Elias, they had been brought there by their father at a young age. How could Jared turn on his family like that? Didn't he care about his brother?

I remembered Mother and her wicked ways.

She'd always treated me poorly, and Grandma often told me it was because Mother was miserable. I'd never understood it. I still didn't. Would Mother have done something like this? Betray her own family? Despite my mixed feelings about her, I liked to think that deep down, she still cared about me.

Maybe one day, if Lyla and Lyson were right about the afterlife, I'd see my family again.

Though I searched the crowd for the blond, bright-eyed twins, they were nowhere to be found. I hoped they were okay. I felt terrible, especially after my awkward interaction with Lyson. He'd tried to kiss me, and I'd pulled away. Was he upset about that? Would he stop talking to me?

"Hey," came a familiar voice.

I turned to find Danika walking next to me. She pulled her red hair behind her back and smiled sweetly at me. Next to her was a young boy—maybe ten or eleven—holding her hand.

The child wasn't hers; she must have been taking care of him. Ever since I'd met Danika in Olympus, she'd always had a unique nurturing vibe. It was only later that I learned how much she cared about children and how devastated she was for having lost several of them to the Elites.

"How you holding up?" she asked.

The young boy watched me closely. "Is that *her*?" he whispered.

By her, I knew he meant, The Girl Who Refused Immortality.

I'd heard the name float around Fort Denton countless times.

"Yes, sweetheart," Danika said, smiling down at him. She turned to me. "I haven't found his father yet. I'm still looking."

I swallowed hard, hoping the boy's father hadn't died in battle.

Next to her, Rose appeared, her glossy brown cheeks forming little hills under her eyes. As usual, she didn't speak, but she smiled at me as a way of saying, *Good to see you.*

I returned the smile.

Beside her was Dax, standing tall as she always did. She walked holding a sharp spear and nudged her chin out at me, a smirk pulling at the corner of her lips.

It was strange to walk alongside my fellow *Breeders.* Not long ago, we'd been sharing a room inside Olympus, destined to breed children for the Elites, or as some people liked to call them, The Immortal Ones.

Although I was exhausted, in pain, and covered in blood, I was thankful to be surrounded by people I'd come to think of as family. For a moment, I forgot about the war, Grandma, and everything. Instead, I smiled at my family around me, thankful.

A warm hand suddenly grabbed mine, and I flinched.

Without a word, Sadie appeared next to me, looking at me with her stunning blue eyes. She smirked and gave my hand a gentle, reassuring squeeze. It was a warm touch that told me, *"We're okay. Everything is okay... We're in this together."*

CHAPTER 4

As we traveled alongside the forest, I felt uneasy. Whenever I spotted a shadow from the corner of my eye, my chest tightened painfully.

The last time we'd traveled this way, a band of criminals with massive guns had robbed us. Machine guns, Reina had called them. Where did those men go? The only relief I felt was knowing I had Sofia by my side. She was one of Elias's best gunwomen, which made me feel safe. And everyone else who held a gun seemed to obey Sofia's orders, which meant she knew what she was doing.

Although I didn't take the time to count, I knew we had at least twelve people armed with guns on our side.

Maybe that alone was enough to keep criminals away from us—the sight of guns.

"You okay?" came Sadie's voice.

It felt like that was all anyone asked me these days—if I was okay.

What kind of question was that? No one was okay. Not with what had just happened.

I couldn't find it in me to lie, so instead, I shrugged.

"Feels like it was all for nothing," I said, staring at the mountains ahead.

"What was?" Sadie asked.

Someone behind us coughed, and Sadie's head shot sideways.

"Going to find the bunker," I said.

She looked at me like I was an idiot.

"Well, think about it," I said. "We moved our people hundreds of miles, and now we're returning from where we came."

Lines formed on her forehead as she gave me a sour look. "Um, yeah, but we now have twice the population we had and more weapons—and we defeated our enemy."

She wasn't wrong.

If it weren't for Elias and his armed soldiers, we might not have defeated the Woodfaces. At least not without losing many people.

The rest of the walk was quiet, aside from children whining or crying. A few rushed through the crowd to come out on the other side to play ball with a young man on the field. It looked like he'd constructed the toy out of leather. He raised his knees, allowing the ball to bounce from one to the other, and the children cheered, some clapping their little hands while others ran in circles as if chasing invisible tails.

As I stared at the grins stretching across their tiny faces, I couldn't help but smile.

Wasn't this what life was about? Finding pleasures, even in darkness? At least, that was what Grandma had always taught me. Even in our lowest moments, she'd find a way to make me smile or even laugh at the silliest thing—like how a drop of spilled soup on the floor had probably put a smile on an ant's face. I remember laughing at the image of an ant smiling.

A few adults joined in on the ball game, and laughter spread throughout the crowd.

It was short-lived, as the playing eventually stopped, and we walked silently for several more hours.

Finally, Ortus's secondary entrance came into view.

To those who knew nothing about Ortus, I imagined it was difficult to believe that a village lay up ahead, behind the giant mountains and leafy trees.

On the left of the mountain cliff was a nearly undetectable path that curved around several hanging branches and two large boulders. The trail was even less visible since Finn had placed broken branches everywhere to protect the remaining survivors inside Ortus.

My heart suddenly skipped a beat.

Darby.

Was she still alive?

I thought of her frail figure, light silvery eyes, and the puffiness that sat beneath them. She had always looked so sickly, and it was no wonder since the woman was allergic to the sun.

I played with the ring on my right hand, twirling it around my third finger. I recalled the L engraving on the inside, which I knew stood for Lillian—Darby's sister.

I still couldn't believe Darby had given me her ring, and now, more than anything, I wanted to be able to give it back to her. I wanted her to be *alive*.

"Whoa," Reina said.

Two horses behind her stood on their hind legs and made loud, frightened noises.

Reina and Maz lunged toward their leather harnesses, pulling on them to try to calm them down.

I rushed to the front of the crowd, carrying my crossbow.

The branches Finn had placed over the path were no longer in position. Someone had dragged them away. Across the two large boulders were bloody handprints smudged, almost as if someone had been too weak to stand straight and had used the boulders for support.

"Let's not jump to conclusions," Finn said.

"Conclusions?" Reina hissed. "Someone's come through here. No one was supposed to come through here."

Whispers broke out through the rest of the crowd as people stood on their tiptoes, trying to see what was causing the sudden stop.

"And my babies sense danger," Maz said, patting one of her horse's necks. "This one here especially." She went on to scratch the white diamond between the horse's eyes.

Finn threw his chin out at Elias, who then whistled at his soldiers. They stampeded toward the front of the crowd, holding on to their shiny metal guns.

"Sweep," Elias ordered.

Finn stood silent, letting Elias take charge of this situation.

But right before Elias and his soldiers entered Ortus, Reina called out, "Wait."

She jumped onto the diamond-faced horse and positioned herself on the saddle. "Let me lead. If you go in there with guns and we still have survivors, some of them may be armed. They'll think you're a threat."

Elias nodded and gave Sofia a look that said, *Do whatever Reina says.*

Sofia, almost twice the height of Reina when on foot, nodded and stepped aside, puffing out her padded chest. She waited until Reina trotted past everyone before ordering the others to follow her closely.

I held my breath, wanting nothing more than to follow Reina inside Ortus.

Finn must have sensed my thoughts. The moment I took a step forward, he stuck his hand out.

"They're fine, Silver. Let's just wait."

The silence was excruciating. I wanted to know what had happened. Who had come this way? And why? If the Woodfaces had followed us to the bunker, then there was no reason for them to have gone to Ortus.

I stared at the bloody smears on the stone.

"Maybe someone changed their mind and tried to follow us to Fort Denton," Sadie said.

I was immediately drawn back into the hospital that rainy night. All around me, pained cries had echoed as people struggled to get some sleep. Our battle against the Woodfaces had caused many deaths and severe injuries. And for those too injured to walk, some chose to stay behind. What if one of the injured ones had changed their mind last minute? What if they'd decided to try to follow us to the bunker?

I stared at the prints.

No. Whoever had come this way went *inside* Ortus. The fingers were pointing in its direction.

Sadie nudged me. "Stop thinking so much. Just be ready."

I loaded my crossbow, and the crowd

behind me started moving. People shuffled from left to right while more and more Champions came to the front, preparing their weapons.

After what we had gone through with the Woodfaces, we were not prepared to go to war again. Worse, we'd spent most of the day walking. I was beyond exhausted and ready to drop into the grass to nap, so I could only imagine how everyone else felt.

I rolled my neck back, feeling a satisfying snap.

When I caught Sadie staring at me, I pointed at her hands with my nose. "Where'd you get that?"

She smiled, twirling a spiked club in her hands. "It was on the ground."

The sharp spikes on it were bloody, and the dark indented handle looked like it had been gripped daily for centuries. I was about to comment on how deadly it looked when a gunshot echoed in the distance.

Several people around us ducked, even though the sound had come from inside Ortus.

"Was that a gun?" Dax asked.

Without thinking, I gripped my crossbow and ran into the village.

CHAPTER 5

Footsteps followed behind me as we charged into the village of Ortus, prepared to fight.

My heart pounded hard inside my chest. Only seconds ago, I'd been exhausted and in pain. But now, as adrenaline pumped through me, I found myself running faster than I ever thought possible.

Countless scenarios played in my mind.

Were there enemies inside the village? Was war breaking out again? Who had fired the shot, anyway? One of ours? Or was there some other armed enemy waiting for us?

I charged up the big hill next to the river, afraid of what I might find on the other side. I wasn't even sure how many people had followed me. I didn't take the time to look back, either.

Just as the burned houses came into view, Reina came trotting toward us on her horse.

With both hands swinging above her head,

she waved at us, her mouth wide and flapping.

What was she doing? Telling us to stop? Or telling us to attack?

She kicked the sides of her horse to move faster toward us.

"Stand down!" she shouted.

This time, I heard her.

I lowered my crossbow and frowned. What was going on? We'd all heard the gunshot. Was anyone injured?

"What's going on?" Sadie asked.

Reina yanked on her horse's reins, trying to reposition the horse sideways. "Accidental discharge."

"What?" I said, not understanding what she was talking about.

"One of the guns," Reina said. "It went off on its own. It's rare, but it happens."

I didn't understand how a gun could fire on its own, but I didn't question her. All that mattered was that everyone was safe.

Reina looked over our heads in the distance and waved an arm—a gesture that I knew meant, *Come in.* I wasn't sure who she had waved at, but it was evident that she was permitting us to enter Ortus.

"Are there survivors?" I asked.

I wanted to ask, Is *Darby alive?* but I kept it to myself.

Reina bowed her head. "A few."

"Lower your weapons," she shouted at

everyone behind me.

A clacking sound echoed as everyone lowered their spears, bows, and other carved weapons. We crept up the hill, some people whispering, but most staying quiet. Many of these people had never seen Ortus before. They'd spent most of their lives underground, living in a bunker.

An uncomfortable silence spread throughout the village when we reached the top of the hill.

Everything was so bare and gray.

The hospital remained, as did the barn and Finn's house, but everything else was nothing more than ash and broken or burned wood. I'd seen the damage before I left, but somehow, it looked worse today. Now that everything had dried, it looked even more depressing.

It reminded me of Lutum—colorless and lifeless.

Even the grass around the homes was gone, leaving nothing but dirt and ash behind.

My throat swelled at the sight.

I'd come to think of this place as home for a while. And now, it was gone.

A warm hand slid across my upper back, and I turned in time to see Finn brushing past me. He offered me a faint smile as if to say, *I know it looks bad, but we'll survive.*

My eyes rolled toward the hundreds of innocent people behind me.

As more and more of them reached the top of the hill, panic began to spread.

"This is where they brought us?" someone said, shocked.

"There are no homes!"

"No shelter," someone added.

"There's that," came a frail voice.

Although I couldn't see the person who'd spoken, I knew they were pointing at the damaged barn.

"Looks like there's food in there," they added.

I was relieved to see that the Woodfaces hadn't come here to destroy what remained. They must have followed us toward the bunker, thinking we'd all left the village.

The crowd began to spread as people ventured off toward the damage, inspecting everything.

I wanted to feel hopeful, but all I felt was dread and defeat.

The sound of a woman crying pulled me out of my darkness. She stood in the distance, near Finn's house, which remained intact on its pillars, and threw her arms around an older man exiting the hospital.

Who was he? Her father?

More people began to reunite, while others searched the village in a panic as if chasing a ghost. I knew many would be left hurting once they found out their loved ones were dead. But before I could dwell on that for too long, someone grabbed my wrist and pulled me away from my friends.

"Pssst," James said.

I stared at my reflection in his sunglasses.

"What?" I whispered back.

He brought me behind the hospital, where it was quiet.

I pulled my wrist out of his grip. "What are you doing?"

"We need to talk," he said.

"Now?" I said, impatient.

He pulled his sunglasses off and placed them on top of his head. "Yes, now."

I dropped my crossbow into the dirt and crossed my arms.

"We need to get back to Lockridge," he said.

I thought of Westin and his father and wondered if they'd ever be reunited again.

"What's the hurry?" I asked. "Westin is for sure still recovering from the gunshot."

"The hurry?" James said as if I hadn't been listening. "The hurry is that I want to get that rover before Jared does."

"The one on the other side of the river?"

He nodded. "If we don't get to it first, Jared will."

"It's out of energy," I pointed out.

James scratched the back of his blond head. "Yeah, that's the tricky part."

"And the ramps are destroyed," I added.

"It's not like we can get across the river."

He waved his hand at me the way Mother used to when she'd lose patience with me. "I know, I know...."

"You either have a plan, or you don't," I said firmly.

He blew air out of his nostrils, calming down. "I'm sorry. I don't have a plan. I'm trying to think of one, and I thought maybe you could help me." He stared at me. "We need that rover, Silver. It could change everything."

I parted my lips to say something along the lines of, *We need a plan first*, when he added, "If we could find a solar panel... I could charge it, and we could drive it back."

I knew what he was talking about because I'd seen solar panels in Fort Denton's courtyard. They'd surprised me at first with their shiny black surfaces and strange wires. It wasn't until I asked someone about them that they told me the panels *collected energy from the sun.*

I had a difficult time wrapping my head around that.

"Where are we supposed to find a solar panel?" I asked.

"Everything okay?" came Dax's voice.

She stood with arms crossed and leaned against the hospital wall, with Danika and Sadie by her side.

Dax gave James a threatening look that told

me she was prepared to handle things physically if he was causing me trouble.

"Everything is okay," I said. "He's on our side."

James slid his sunglasses back on like he always did when other people were around. It was as if this brought him comfort in social settings.

"I'll catch you later, Silver."

I almost argued and demanded that we figure this out now, but my friends were looking at me funny. Danika played with the tips of her red hair and made her eyes go big as if to say, *Well, you coming?*

"What's going on?" I asked.

"Finn's about to make a speech," Sadie said. "He wants everyone there."

Although she was talking to me, she kept her eyes glued on James as he walked by her. It wasn't jealousy, but it wasn't kindness, either. It was like she didn't trust him. And I didn't blame her, either. Sadie still didn't know what had happened at that farmhouse. She wasn't aware that Jared had tried to kill us or that I'd almost drowned in the river on the way back.

We all stared at each other for a moment. It was as if they were waiting for me to tell them about my chat.

I cleared my throat. "Have any of you seen Asako?"

Dax and Danika exchanged a look.

"I did," Danika said. "She's in one of the carts." She pointed in the general direction of where we'd come from. "They're having a hard time getting her out."

"What do you mean?" I asked.

Asako was a small woman. She may have weighed as much as a child.

"She doesn't want to come out," Dax said. "She's terrified."

"Then what are we doing here?" I asked matter-of-factly. "She's probably scared because she's been through a lot, and now she's in some strange place where she doesn't know anyone."

I didn't give anyone the time to argue with me.

Rushing past them, I jogged around the crowd forming in front of Finn's house.

CHAPTER 6

I didn't recognize her.

When I'd met her in Olympus, Asako had always been straightforward and unhumorous. I never heard her laugh, and she rarely smiled. Once, when Star had made a joke, Asako had smirked in the shadows.

But this woman in the corner looked nothing like the Asako I had known. She seemed almost wild, sitting with her shoulders slouched forward, her knees bent, and her arms wrapped around her legs.

I stepped closer, resting my palms against the wood of the cart. As I stared at her, the scent of damp wood and dirt filled my nostrils.

Her hair, scraggly black strings, draped all over her sallow skin, sticking to it. She wore some sort of white garment—maybe a hospital robe—but most of it was strained gray, brown, and black, as was her skin.

It made me feel terrible.

Guilty, even.

As if reading my mind, Dax wrapped an arm around my shoulder. "We didn't do this, Silver. And I told you the nurses wouldn't let me in to see her while we were in the bunker. Remember? It's not like we didn't try."

I didn't remember.

I'd been so preoccupied with everything else that I'd pushed Asako to the back of my mind.

"I tried too," Danika said. "The nurses kept saying she wasn't ready to socialize."

When I didn't say anything, Dax pulled her arm away and patted my back. "You had a lot going on, Silver. You still do. You can't be responsible for everyone."

Swallowing my guilt, I climbed up into the cart with Dax's help. She hopped in next, causing the whole thing to shift and creak.

Behind Sadie were two nurses eyeing us carefully. They whispered back and forth, making me feel like they didn't trust us near Asako.

"They'll be fine," Danika assured them.

"We have sedation ready," said one of the nurses.

Danika flicked her wrist. "You won't be needing that."

One slow step at a time, I moved closer to Asako. Every few seconds, she turned her head sideways to look at us but quickly jerked the other way, causing her hair to fall back over her eyes.

"Hey, Asako," I said softly. "It's me, Silver. Remember? From Olympus?"

Her dark eyes rolled my way. She looked at me, then Dax, then at Danika behind us.

I turned around and gestured for Danika to join. With Sadie's help, she climbed up and met us at the halfway point.

"Hey, Asako," Danika tried.

The wood beneath our feet creaked, and Asako's eyes widened at us. Then, for a split second, she bared her teeth at us like a rabid wolf. It was strange to see a human acting this way. What had the Woodfaces done to her?

She wrapped her arms around her legs again, and only then did I see the scars. Some were long and straight, and others circular and uneven. They ran down her left arm, and although I couldn't see her right arm, I imagined the scars were similar on that side, too. It looked like someone had taken a sharp object and intentionally carved her skin.

The scars were pink and bubbly, some even red and scabby, which told me she was still healing. Her fingernails were black and indented, and she dug them into her meatless legs.

Asako had always been petite, but she'd lost so much weight that she now resembled a skeleton wearing a skinsuit.

"Do you remember us?" I asked.

Her eyes lingered on me and then on Dax and Danika.

She gave us a brief nod.

I wanted to smile at the progress, but I didn't. We were only getting started.

Asako bared her teeth again when I took another step and started kicking at the cart's base. It was like she was trying to back up even farther, but all it did was push her into the corner again and again.

"Hey, hun," came Danika's sweet voice. "It's us, remember? Your sisters."

Asako made a hissing sound through her front teeth. It was apparent that even though she recognized us, she felt threatened.

"What did they do to her?" Dax whispered, her head turning sideways.

"Hey," I said as softly as I could.

Carefully, I knelt in front of her, and she pulled her head back so far it hit the wood behind her.

"I'm not here to hurt you," I said. "Do you remember being in Olympus?"

She stared at me for a moment and nodded.

That was progress. At least she remembered.

"Do you remember the train?" I asked.

Again, she nodded.

"Me too," I said, touching my chest. "They threw me out, and I got injured. I bet you got injured, too."

She nodded again.

Then, her eyes got big, like she was looking for someone. She swayed her head from side to side, damp black hair clinging to her cheeks.

"Who are you looking for?" I asked.

But the sadness in her eyes told me who she was looking for.

Star and Echo... Our other friends.

"They're gone," I said.

I wanted to reach out and console her, but I was afraid she might try to attack me if I touched her.

"I-I'm sorry," I added.

She looked away from me.

"But we're here," Danika said, stepping closer to me. "And we want to help. Please, Asako. Let us help you."

Asako's eyes glazed over like she was somewhere else. What was she thinking about? The torment the Woodfaces had put her through?

There was so much I wanted to know, but it was apparent she wasn't ready to talk about it.

"I'm sorry the Woodfaces hurt you," I said.

"H-h-hurt?" Asako asked, looking confused.

Had they brainwashed her? I pointed at the scars across her arms and face. "Yes, hurt," I said. "They took you as a prisoner. Don't you remember? Elias is the only reason you're here."

She pulled her face back like I was speaking in a different language.

"They..." She swallowed hard, and it looked painful. "Did not. They... They didn't hurt me."

I looked over at Dax and Danika, who looked as confused as I felt.

Did Asako not realize she was cut up everywhere? Or, did she not remember what they'd done to her?

I leaned in a bit closer.

"Asako, you're all scarred up."

She scowled at me, and I wondered if kneeling had been a mistake.

"The Woodfaces didn't—" but she stopped herself and breathed out hard through her flared little nostrils. She tightened her colorless lips, almost like she was trying to hold in an explosion.

"The Woodfaces..." she said, her eyes glazing over again.

She was gone once more—lost in her memories.

"Asako." I reached for her shoulder, and she flinched so hard that I jumped back.

"I'm sorry," I blurted, keeping my hand to myself.

Her dark eyes zeroed in on me so intently that I got the feeling she was preparing to lunge at me—to grab me by the throat and not let go until I died. Why was she so furious? Was it because I touched her?

"The Woodfaces are not bad," she said through gritted teeth.

I couldn't help but frown. Her words angered me so much that I almost got up and walked away. We'd lost countless people to the Woodfaces, and I'd nearly lost Sadie. How could she sit there and tell me that the Woodfaces weren't bad? They were the enemy. They had come after us, wanting blood. They'd even used Asako as leverage by threatening to kill her in front of us.

"They almost killed you," I said, clenching my teeth.

Asako rolled her eyes and shook her head from side to side. It was a slow movement that made me feel like a child—like someone who simply didn't understand anything.

"Would you tell us what's going on?" I said. "You're acting like the Woodfaces are good people. Like they saved you, or something—"

I was about to add, "When in reality, they wanted to kill you," but she suddenly shifted from her position with tight, white-knuckled fists.

"Because they did save me!" she shouted at me, her eyes as dark as coal.

CHAPTER 7

I wiped Asako's saliva from my chin and backed away, confused.

Then, her eyes widened, and her breath quickened. Every few seconds, she sucked in a lungful of air as if drowning. What was going on? Why did she look like that? So afraid? So—

"Move," Danika ordered.

It wasn't like Danika to order anyone around. But Danika was empathetic; whenever someone was suffering, she never hesitated to take action. It was as if in an instant, she knew exactly what needed to be done and wasn't afraid to tell others what to do.

We stepped aside as she came in close to Asako.

"It's okay," she said, touching Asako's shoulder.

I cringed at the sight of it, imagining what Asako might do to her if she felt threatened. She'd lived among Woodfaces for weeks, as far as I knew. And with how cut up she was, she was likely traumatized, which made her dangerous.

Asako's breathing heightened in pitch, like her throat was constricting.

I wanted to ask what was going on, but Danika quickly said, "Both of you, get off the cart."

"What—" Dax said.

"She's having a panic attack," Danika said. "Give us some space."

"A panic—" I said, wanting more information on this strange term.

But Dax nudged me and said, "Let's go."

I followed her to the end of the cart and jumped off, landing right next to Sadie.

"What's going on?" Sadie asked.

"A panicked attack or something," Dax said.

"Panic attack," Sadie corrected her.

I raised an eyebrow at her. She knew what this was? Was this something everyone was familiar with? I felt like a true citizen of Lutum again—someone who lacked basic knowledge. As grateful as I was for the education Grandma gave me through books and personal stories, it didn't replace living and breathing in the real world.

"What?" Sadie said. "You've never seen someone have a panic attack?"

Both Dax and I shook our heads.

"Is it an illness?" I asked.

Sadie shrugged. "Um, sometimes. It's

anxiety. Some people have it worse than others. And sometimes, it comes out of nowhere. Other times, it's caused by something traumatic—" She paused, her eyes wandering toward the ground.

"Can it hurt her?" I asked.

Sadie snapped back to reality. "No... not really. It's a horrible feeling that makes you feel like you're dying, but it doesn't actually hurt you. At least not physically."

As I stared at Asako at the other end of the cart, I hoped to never experience a *panic attack*.

She breathed in hard as if her lungs were failing her. But Danika kept comforting her, whispering things in her ear. Eventually, she stopped gasping for air and went so quiet I wondered if she'd died in a seated position.

I stared at her, waiting for her to move.

"Is she—" I started.

"Asako?" Danika said, gently shaking her shoulder.

But Asako was staring off at the cart's wooden side wall. Why wasn't she moving? Where had she gone?

"Asako?" Danika repeated.

When Asako didn't budge, Danika looked at us and shrugged. It was a look that told me she'd done everything she knew how to do, but Asako's new state was something she'd never seen before.

"Asako!" Danika tried once more, this time shaking her.

Without warning, Asako let out a broken scream and hurled herself on top of Danika.

"Shit," Dax mumbled, stumbling as she climbed back into the cart.

Sadie and I jumped in after her.

At the other end of the cart, Asako sat on top of Danika with fingers wrapped around her throat. She kept screaming in Danika's face as she strangled her. Squiggly veins zigzagged across Asako's forehead as she used all her strength to strangle Danika. Underneath her, Danika's face mirrored Asako's—dark red, bulging veins, big eyes—but for a different reason; she couldn't breathe.

"Get off of her!" Dax shouted, her voice deep and authoritative.

She grabbed Asako around the armpits, but Asako swung back, catching Dax in the nose.

Dax reached for her nose, then pulled her fingers back, checking for blood.

At the same time, I lunged for Asako's other side and tried to drag her off Danika.

But she was too strong. How was she this strong? Asako was half Dax's size and smaller than me, and the two of us combined should have been enough to remove her.

Dax gave me a look that I knew translated to, *Let's do this at the same time.*

Without delay, I nodded, and we hurried

toward Asako, locking her arms against our chests.

Sadie joined in, helping us pin her to the cart's uneven floor.

With her arms pinned, Asako started kicking and screaming, her matted black hair masking her sunken red face. Strands even slipped into her wide, open mouth, but she didn't seem to care.

Danika was too disoriented to help. She crawled backward and reached for her swollen neck, but not in time. Asako kicked so hard she knocked Danika in the face, sending her head rolling back.

"Get her legs!" Dax shouted.

Sadie jumped on Asako, pinning her legs down.

At the other end of the cart, the two nurses who had allowed us to see Asako hurried up into the cart. The one on the left—a young, dark-skinned woman with fear in her eyes—extracted something from her pocket. Her hands shook as she prepared a syringe. It was as if she'd never done this before. The other nurse, slightly older and calmer-looking, reassured her while giving her clear instructions.

The younger nurse nodded, rushed toward us, and dropped to her knees.

Without hesitating, she jabbed the needle into Asako's arm and pressed down on something.

Within seconds, Asako stopped kicking, and her muscles relaxed.

Watching us, she licked her dry, cracked lips, her eyes rolling from side to side.

"D-D-D—" she tried.

I leaned in, wanting to hear more.

Her eyelids fluttered, and she fell unconscious, her head rolling to the side.

CHAPTER 8

The crowd in front of Finn's house became so thick I wondered if we'd even make it to the hospital.

Not only did I want to check in on Asako, but I also wanted to see if Darby was in there—if she was still alive.

"This way," Dax said, forcing her way through countless people.

I followed Dax with Sadie and Danika right behind me. When we reached the hospital's front doors, a nurse at the front stuck out her hand.

"I'm sorry, but we're at capacity," she said.

"We're just visiting," I said.

She shook her head. "Even for visitors. With all of the injuries, there's no space. I'm sorry."

I craned my neck to peek inside, but all I saw were blue curtains everywhere. Now and then, white coats rushed by. It didn't matter that I couldn't see the chaos—I could *hear* it.

People moaned in pain, and others cried

out. Some even angrily shouted at nurses and doctors, demanding pain medication.

"Are these all new patients?" I asked.

The nurse looked at me curiously, no doubt sensing I was fishing for information. But the stare didn't last long. Her eyes darted from side to side, and she stepped toward us.

"Most are from today's injuries. We're also taking care of Harley—"

"Harley?" I asked, scrunching my nose.

"Didn't you hear?" she said. "He's the one who tried to follow you… to follow his wife and children after everyone left searching for the bunker. His stitches came undone as he ran. He almost bled to death. Thankfully, he came back here for care."

"The handprints," I mumbled to myself. "D-did he get to see his wife and children again?"

A gentle smirk pulled at her lips. "He did. And he's recovering now."

I felt awful at the thought of this poor man chasing after his family, barely hanging on to life. But I was thankful to know he'd been reunited with his loved ones.

The nurse crossed her arms. "We also have a few people in here due to malnutrition…" She paused like she was waiting for us to figure it out.

"People who stayed behind," I finally said.
She nodded.

This didn't surprise me. Most people who

had stayed behind were either ill, injured, or severely disabled. How had anyone expected them to feed themselves? A few nurses and doctors had stayed behind, but obviously, it hadn't been enough.

I parted my lips, prepared to ask her if Darby was in there, when Finn's loud voice echoed across Ortus.

"People of Ortus and Fort Denton," he shouted.

He stood halfway up the stairs to his home, using the right railing for support. He looked tired and defeated, like all he wanted to do was finish the climb and go to sleep in his house.

Next to him, Elias stood with his chest puffed out and his hands gripping his hips. He watched his people but didn't say a word. He didn't have to. The confidence he exuded proved to me that he trusted Finn.

The whispering around me became quieter as people listened.

"Today has not been easy for any of us," he continued. "We have all lost our home; for some of you, this home was the only place you knew. Then, I bring you all here, to an unfamiliar place—or an old home, for some of you—that was demolished by Woodfaces."

A few gasps spread throughout the crowd. For some, the term Woodface was something they'd learned only today, after the attack. I imagined the name itself was enough to bring about fear.

"While I can't promise you safety from the Elites here, what I can do is make sure everyone gets fed and has a place to sleep tonight."

The crowd didn't seem satisfied with Finn's words. Feet shuffled, whispers broke out, and scowls appeared all around me.

I didn't blame them.

How could I?

Finn wasn't giving anyone hope.

And after everything these people had gone through, all they wanted was to feel safe—probably more than they wanted food and a bed.

I always appreciated Finn's honesty, but as I stared at the frightened faces around me—some young and covered in blood, others old and wrinkled—I knew they needed to hear something else.

Something *more*.

"Excuse me," I mumbled, forcing my way through the crowd.

"Silver!" Sadie hissed behind me.

There was no telling when we'd find each other again, especially with such a large population now. But something inside me told me I had to say something. I wasn't even sure Finn would let me up his stairs, and part of me didn't want to do this. I wasn't some leader. It wasn't my responsibility.

But at that moment, it felt wrong not to say anything.

When I reached the bottom of Finn's long, exterior staircase, Reina watched me curiously. She didn't block my way up or ask me what I was doing—it was almost like she trusted me enough not to ask questions.

As I climbed up, one tired step at a time, the crowd went quiet.

Finn paused, watching me, and next to him, Elias stood silent.

I wasn't sure if Elias had been preparing to speak next, and the thought suddenly made me feel stupid. What if he'd been about to calm the people of Ortus and Fort Denton? As I continued my climb, I considered turning back around. But if I did that, I'd look stupid. Everyone's eyes were on me. I could feel it.

But then, my mind started racing. What if my appearance made things worse? After all, the Woodfaces had wanted *me*.

No, I quickly argued with myself. *Jared set this up. They entered the courtyard, prepared to kill everyone. They didn't even ask for you.*

When I reached the halfway point, Finn patted me on the shoulder as if to say, *Welcome.*

Elias gave me a brief nod and a smile that seemed like a chore for him. The bags under his eyes told me he was beyond exhausted, and how he kept shifting his body weight told me he was in pain.

Slowly, I turned around to face the hundreds of eyes focused on me.

I swallowed hard. "I-I," I mumbled.

But when I saw a few friendly faces nodding at me—Rose, James, Lyson—I cleared my throat. "I know for some of you, this has been the worst day of your life."

Some people bowed their heads, while others looked away.

"Families have been separated," I continued. "Many people have been injured or worse, killed."

Two women sobbed in the background, and I felt awful for having brought up those we'd lost. Although I was thankful that gun-wielding fighters had saved most of us, a few hadn't been so lucky.

"I know this place doesn't look like much right now." I pointed my chin at the village or what remained of it. "But I know how resilient you all are. I've seen how hard you all work. I've seen you all come together. I've seen you adapt to living with an entirely new society. And I know that if we work hard together, we can rebuild this village and make it a place for you to call home."

Many people nodded, but a few scowls remained.

I parted my lips to keep going when someone shouted, "Why are you even talking to us? You're the reason we're here!"

The crowd blew up—some defending me, others agreeing with this faceless voice.

"And she's the reason that Eye thing came over our village in the first place!"

I looked down at Sadie, my stomach sinking.

Although I wanted to argue and blame the Elites for this, I couldn't. Deep down, I agreed with these people. I knew it wasn't my fault, and I hadn't *intentionally* caused any of this, but the truth was that their lives were in danger so long as I stayed there.

"You're right," I said.

The bickering stopped instantly, and confused gazes spread through the crowd.

"You're absolutely right," I repeated. "I'm the one the Elites want. Not you. And so long as I stay here, you're all in danger."

Finn took a step toward me, but I stuck out my hand, gesturing at him to let me continue.

Below, Sadie's brows came close together like she was trying to tell me to stop talking. If she'd been standing next to me, she would have probably said something like, "What the hell are you doing? Stop it."

Either that, or she would have tugged at my arm, urging me to stop.

But I couldn't stop.

I had to do what was right.

And right now, staying here wasn't right.

Not after two wars only weeks apart.

The Elites wanted *me*, and everyone knew it.

We'd stayed safe underground for a while, away from the Elites' line of vision. But now, we were out in the open. Although Finn was right to feel safe between the mountains, it didn't protect us from Eyes circling over our heads, searching for me.

And maybe the next time this happened, these Eyes would be equipped with dangerous weapons capable of destroying our entire village within seconds.

Now that I knew about machine guns, imagining them attached to a flying drone wasn't so far-fetched.

Gripping the wooden railing next to me, I took a step down, away from Finn. "The only way you will be safe is if I'm gone. At least for a while."

In the crowd, Sadie shook her head at me, devastated.

And as much as I wanted to apologize to her, I couldn't.

"Tomorrow morning," I said, "I leave Ortus."

CHAPTER 9

Silver," Finn hissed as I took another step down the stairs.

The crowd blew up again, and people started shouting back and forth. It became so loud I couldn't hear my own footsteps against the wood.

"You don't have to do this," Finn said.

He tried to follow me, but Elias grabbed his shoulder. "Maybe it's for the best."

Finn pulled away from him and followed me as I descended the stairs.

"Silver, please," Finn tried. "These people need you."

I stopped near the end of the staircase to look at him.

"These people don't need *me*. They need guidance and hope," I said. "You can give them that." I paused and looked up at Elias. "You can *both* give them that."

"You *are* their hope, Silver," Finn said. "You've shown the world that we can stand up to corruption."

"Danger also follows me everywhere."

Finn swallowed. He couldn't argue.

"If the Elites find you out there, they'll kill you," he said.

When I reached the bottom of the staircase, Reina was waiting with a smirk on her face.

"Always the brave one," she said.

I almost scoffed but held it in. I didn't feel brave. If anything, I was terrified. I didn't want to leave, but I also didn't want to be the cause of another war.

"If the Eye doesn't come while I'm gone, I'll assume it's safe for me to return," I said.

"Silver!" Sadie shouted, running toward me.

Behind her were Dax and Danika.

"What the hell was that about?" Sadie asked.

I smiled at her—not because anything was funny, but because I was right about how she'd react.

She scowled even harder. "Is something funny?"

I shook my head. "No—"

"Silver!" James called out. He ran toward me, looking happier than ever, and wrapped his arms around Dax and Sadie. As he ran, his red-framed sunglasses fell out of his blond hair and landed on the bridge of his nose.

He grinned at me.

Sadie was the first to pull away, looking disgusted. He smiled over at Dax, who slowly pulled his arm off her shoulder as if it were covered in mold.

"Quite a bold move you made there," he said, still smiling.

No one seemed to understand what he was so happy about.

But I did.

"So?" he asked, his blond—almost white—brows appearing higher than his *shades*, as he liked to call them.

I glanced awkwardly at everyone around me. They were all waiting for an answer. But what was I supposed to tell them? The truth?

Then I realized something: Jared was no longer in the picture, so keeping secrets didn't matter anymore. Who was I protecting by telling them about the rover?

"We left a rover on the other side of the river," I said bluntly.

A few eyes blinked, and Finn stood with his mouth open.

"If we can get it up and running, we can keep doing our wheat runs," I said.

"But how?" Elias asked. "There's no power here." He stuck his arms out to emphasize how bare the village was and how we had no source of electricity.

Finn's eyes shot up at the curious crowd behind us. Some were so intrigued with what we were talking about that they'd taken several steps closer, nearly shoulder to shoulder with Dax.

"Why don't we take this conversation somewhere else?" Finn asked.

I nodded and followed him up into his house. Beside me, James looked as excited as ever. I kept giving him a cold stare to remind him to keep Lockridge out of the conversation.

It wasn't that I didn't trust Finn or Reina or my friends; I wasn't yet to break my promise to Ari. I'd told her that I would keep Lockridge a secret.

James, so far, had kept his mouth shut about the whole thing, and I respected him for that. I only hoped he could keep things quiet a little longer.

When we entered Finn's home, it was quiet and gloomy. The deeper we went, the dirtier it became. Some survivors who had stayed behind had decided to move in there.

Dirty dishes sat across his kitchen counter, and muddy footprints covered the wooden plank boards. Although I could tell it bothered Finn—his lip kept twitching on one side—he didn't make it obvious.

Most of us sat around the kitchen table— the same one we'd sat around when trying to come up with a plan to leave Ortus. Only this time, its surface looked sticky with coffee and food stains.

Everyone stared at the mess, but no one said anything. It was like everyone was sharing the same thought: life in Ortus hadn't been easy after most of the population left.

"The rover," Elias said, aiming his gaze at James. "Is it the R-789?"

James nodded.

I wasn't sure what that meant, but I was glad James spoke Elias's language.

Elias scratched at his fully grown salt-and-pepper beard, nodding slowly. Today, his medium-length hair was tied back, causing his dark curls to flatten. He didn't tie it often—it usually hung in waves, constantly looking wet—but the tied look suited him, too.

He sat next to Finn, a few inches shorter, and leaned forward, his bulky arms masking a brown stain.

"We need a Z model solar panel to power that thing. The old-school ones won't cut it."

Everyone stared at them as though they were speaking a different language.

James smiled at Elias like he had some big secret.

What did he have to smile about?

"The courtyard," they said at the same time.

"The one above the stable," James clarified. "I remember when you guys found that thing and said it was as strong as twenty combined."

Elias patted James on the shoulder, and James's glasses almost fell off his face.

"Good memory, my boy," Elias said.

Finding this solar panel must have been an enormous deal for Fort Denton. No wonder James had remembered its exact location.

"So you want us to go back to Fort Denton and steal one of their solar panels?" I asked.

Everyone paused, probably realizing how awful that sounded.

"What about the innocent people there? Don't they rely on this power?" I asked.

"We did," Elias said, "but we also survived for years without it. And now, half of Fort Denton's population is here. If we don't get that rover, we don't get the wheat. That vehicle is the only thing that can make it over the river without us having to build a bridge."

"We'd still need to build a ramp," James said.

Elias looked at him like he was waiting for more information. When James didn't say anything else, Elias flicked his hand out as if to say, *That's no big deal.*

"You kids managed to do it in a day," Elias said. "I'm sure you can figure something out."

"Elias is right," Reina cut in. Her already narrowed eyes got even smaller as she stared at the coffee stains, lost in thought. I was happy to see her back in her combat clothing—green cotton, black shoulder pads, a weapons belt, and shiny leather boots. Unlike the other Champions, Reina wore a few shiny pins over her left breast. I wasn't sure what they represented, but I knew they had something to do with her being the General of our Champions. She always seemed to have more confidence when she wore them.

"We've lost half our food supply in the barn," she said, and paused. She clenched her teeth, causing her already square jaw to look even sharper. Sighing, she added, "It'll take months for new crops."

"What?" I blurted. "How did that happen?"

Reina looked at Finn with sadness in her eyes. "Part of the barn's roof collapsed. The damage didn't look bad when we left Ortus, but it was worse than we thought. I guess all that rain caused a bunch of damage."

Before anyone could react negatively, Elias cut in. "And this is why these two will get that rover back up and running. We'll be able to do some wheat runs again."

"Make that three," Sadie said.

She stepped in under the light, her dark blue eyes looking a little brighter today.

"No, Sadie—" I tried.

"Three it is," Reina said.

It was no use arguing. Sadie was Reina's favorite Champion.

"Four," Dax said.

I sighed. As much as I appreciated my friends wanting to help, I didn't want to put them in danger.

"Oh, don't act like you've got this under control," Sadie said, poking me hard in the back. "I'm the one who taught you how to fight, remember?"

I smirked. She wasn't wrong. Even though I'd learned how to use weapons, Sadie had been training far longer than I had.

Dax stood proudly next to Sadie and ran a hand through her short brown hair, then gave Danika a crooked smile and said, "Five?"

Everyone looked at Danika.

It took a few seconds for her to realize the attention was on her, and when she did, she laughed out loud. "Yeah, no. I'm not going. Are you kidding?" I was happy to see she still had her feisty personality. "I can't fight. I'll stay here and help look after the kids."

Dax nudged her playfully, then wrapped an arm around her. "I'm only teasing you."

Danika gave her a flat-lidded look, but after a pause, she smiled back.

"Then it's settled," Elias said. He clapped his hands together and stood, his chair scraping the floor.

His voice echoed throughout Finn's house, and as he stood between his chair and the table, smiling at everyone, I wondered how well he would fit into Ortus. Finn was the leader, not Elias, but by the way Elias carried himself, it looked like he wanted to be in charge.

I only hoped it wouldn't lead to any problems.

Before Finn could say anything, Elias cheerfully said, "Let's get you prepared for your travels!"

CHAPTER 10

expect them back in full health," Maz said, her tone threatening.

I couldn't tell if she was wishing us good luck or if she only cared that we came back with her horses.

Maybe a little bit of both.

I stared over the fence separating the training grounds from the village, admiring the bright blue sky. Although we had intended to leave first thing in the morning, we'd all slept in to catch up on some much-needed rest.

I admired the sky and the few white tufts of clouds floating by. It was a much-needed beauty, especially after my awful night. Not only had I discovered that Darby had passed away after we left, but I'd slept on Finn's floor atop a pile of moist hay. It was painful compared to the bed I'd grown to love in the bunker.

I focused on Maz as she prepared the three horses for our travels. She fastened saddles around them and slipped bridles onto their faces. Although she was short and had to stand on the tips of her toes to get the saddles on their backs, she did it easily. When her sleeves rolled back, revealing her countless pink scars from dog bites, she didn't seem to care.

Maz always displayed her scars proudly. I imagined for her, it was proof that she'd stop at nothing to train her animals.

The biggest of the horses—the one she called Bumpy—stood quietly, chewing tall grass as she threw a two-person saddle on his back. His brown coat looked filthy, probably because Maz hadn't groomed him in a while.

Maz had always spent hours taking care of the horses and her dogs. Not long ago, she'd lost one of her dogs to some illness. It devastated her, and she'd stopped coming out into the courtyard until the day of the attack. That was the first day she came back out.

Although she seemed a bit angrier than usual today, I was happy to see her returning to her normal self.

"This should tide you over for a week." She handed us a big forest green bag that matched the Champion clothing I was now wearing.

"What is it?" I asked, trying to peek inside.

Ignoring me, she fastened it to a horse's saddle.

"Food, water," Sadie said, then eyeballed Maz. "I think."

I glanced at the half-burned stable, feeling bad for Maz. How long would it take them to rebuild it?

Fortunately, the training field was mostly empty, aside from a handful of Champions who appeared to be releasing some anger by throwing spears into wooden targets. Most Champions were too exhausted to train right now and, instead, had found somewhere cozy to lie down.

"If you plan on returning," Maz said, her gaze falling on me, "be sure to have something worthwhile."

What did that even mean?

I must have been giving her a funny look, because her eyelids went flat like she was annoyed at having to re-explain herself. "You told everyone you're leaving for our safety, but it looks more like you're going on a mission to me. So if you're coming back with them"—she wiggled a finger at Dax, Sadie, and James—"you'd better come back with something special enough that the people will forget why you left in the first place."

"I'm not coming back if it's going to risk—"

Maz waved a hand in front of her face to quiet me.

It worked.

She wasn't the type to use many words, and I imagined that was because she spent so much time around animals every day and didn't much care to socialize with humans.

"I'm only doing my job by helping you survive out there," she said. "I don't need to hear any details or your life story."

Finally, she stood straight and smacked her hands together, causing dirt particles to float between us. "You're all set."

"Thanks, Maz—" I tried, but she spun around and left the stables.

"What's her problem?" I asked.

Sadie gave me a look with raised eyebrows. "Seriously? She lost half her animals, Silver. Show a little compassion."

"Oh," was all I could think to say.

I'd been so preoccupied with the idea of leaving Ortus that I'd forgotten about Jared's awful deal. As I watched Maz go with her broad shoulders swaying from side to side, I suddenly felt guilty.

"Don't," Sadie said, jabbing me in the arm.

"What?" I blurted.

"Don't get in your head," she said. "Don't start blaming yourself. Jared did this. Not you."

She was right.

Clearing my throat, I pointed at the two-person saddle and then at James. "I'm guessing that's for you."

He slid sunglasses down the bridge of his nose and inspected the horse. "The two-seater? Yep. Definitely. I can't drive these things."

Sadie rolled her eyes. "You don't drive. Never mind. Come here. I'll help you up."

It was funny to watch James climb onto the horse. He seemed nervous—a look that didn't suit him. His hair wiggled atop his head as he fought to pull himself up. When he was finally up, he still looked entirely out of his element.

"This thing gonna fall sideways?" he asked, shifting from side to side in the saddle.

Sadie stepped toward the horse and tugged hard on the leather straps under the horse's belly.

"No," she confirmed.

"So it's never happened?" he yelled as though far away from us, making the whole thing even funnier. I supposed he wasn't used to sitting so high up.

"I didn't say that," Sadie said. "Of course, it's happened."

His mouth hung open for a moment. "What? Why didn't you tell me? Why don't we have headgear? I mean, one kick from this horse, and I could go flying. I could injure my spine and lose the ability to walk. I could—"

"James," I said sternly.

He stopped talking and cleared his throat.

"I know this isn't your rover, and you have to put your faith in an animal, but you'll be fine. Especially with Sadie leading the way."

I smirked and patted Sadie's back.

"What?" Sadie blurted. "No. I'm not—"

Before giving her time to argue, I climbed on the second horse—a gorgeous black creature with a white belly—and Dax climbed onto the third one.

Sadie released a sharp sigh, fastened her long brown hair into a ponytail, and said, "Whatever."

I smiled back at Dax as Sadie climbed onto the horse with James. She swung her long leg over his head to climb on, and James ducked just in time.

"Whoa, watch it," he said. "You almost hit my glasses!"

Without looking back, Sadie said, "If you're going to be whiny, you're staying here. Got it?"

It reminded me of the Sadie I'd first met.

He nodded fast, and with trembling hands, positioned his crooked sunglasses back on his face.

"Hold on," she ordered.

"T-to what?" he said, his voice shrill.

He looked at me for guidance, so I pointed at the little leather handle behind Sadie's butt. It wasn't much, and it certainly wasn't as handy as the knob she had at the front—or the *pummel*, as she'd taught me—but it was better than nothing.

"Your other option is to hold on to me," Sadie said.

"This is fine," James said.

Before he could say another word, Sadie

kicked the sides of her horse, and off they went, with James leaning back so far I wondered if he might fall off.

Dax and I watched as they trotted around the wooden fence while James held on to his sunglasses for dear life.

CHAPTER 11

James swayed from side to side behind Sadie as she led us along the forest by the river. The last time we'd traveled this way, a bunch of men with machine guns had robbed us.

Maybe this wasn't the safest path.

Every now and then, Sadie snapped her head back to speak to James. Although I couldn't hear them from this distance, it looked like she was scolding him for either talking too much or not giving proper directions.

Dax let out a soft chuckle, so I looked at her.

"They don't exactly make a strong team," she said. "Why didn't you ride with James?"

"I-I don't know," I said.

The truth was, I did know. Deep down, I was afraid that if James and I kept being friends, he'd try something like Lyson had tried in the library—he'd try to kiss me. And I wasn't interested in him like that.

I felt stupid for even having the thought.

Who was to say James thought of me in that way at all? He'd never made any comments about me being pretty or anything.

Sighing, I stared at the sky, wishing Grandma could tell me how to act better around people. She always seemed to have so much experience interacting with others.

"Sadie's doing fine," I said.

"Sadie can't stand the guy," Dax said.

James slumped his shoulders and sat quietly, which wasn't like him. I wondered what Sadie had told him. Probably something like *Shut up* or *Sit still and shut that hole in your face.* She could be cold sometimes, especially with people she didn't know.

"How's Mia feel about you coming along?" I asked, changing the subject.

Dax and Mia had gotten close since they met inside Fort Denton. I often saw them holding hands or walking side by side with Dax's long arm around Mia's shoulder.

Dax looked down at her saddle and shrugged. "Wasn't too happy about it."

"Well, she's probably scared," I said.

Dax nodded. "She is."

I parted my lips to say something like, *Well, she cares about you,* when a pained grunt escaped the forest next to us.

I tugged at my reins, ordering my horse to stop. Dax did the same while Sadie kept moving. She probably hadn't heard anything since she'd been too busy bickering with James.

"Sadie," I whispered sharply.

She snapped her head sideways. When she saw me looking at the forest with big eyes, she turned around and threw her chin out at me as if to say, *What is it?*

I pointed at my ear and then at the forest.

Again, that same noise escaped the forest's darkness.

It sounded human—a man's voice, a deep lament.

Scowling, I jumped off my horse and grabbed my spear. The others followed close behind, their feet landing softly in the grass.

I led the way, the tip of my stone spear aimed at the forest trees.

The sound grew louder as we approached, but the hidden man went quiet when I stepped on a twig. Had he heard us? Was this a trap? Was I being stupid by going straight into the unknown?

Something shuffled nearby, and then I saw movement. It hadn't been fast, but it was low to the ground—it almost looked like someone trying to crawl into a pile of leaves.

I aimed my spear at the dark figure on the ground and looked at the others.

Everyone nodded and moved in closer.

Next to a thick tree with protruding roots was a man dressed in black from head to toe.

On his head was a black cotton hat that sat crookedly, on the verge of falling off his head. Blood speckles ran across his brown stubbly face and neck. He held two trembling and bloody hands next to his face.

"P-p-please," he begged, now lying flat on his back.

He'd tried to cover himself up with leaves and branches, but he was trembling so badly that leaves kept slipping through his fingers.

"Who are you?" I asked.

His flat-lidded eyes darted between me and the others. He looked exhausted. When he didn't answer, Sadie stepped forward, her spear beside mine.

The man gulped and cleared his throat. "S-S-Samesh," he said.

"Samesh," I repeated. "Why are you here? What happened to you?"

His face looked familiar, but I couldn't figure out where I knew him from. Or, as Grandma used to say, I *couldn't put my finger on it.*

Had he come from the bunker? His black clothes gave me that impression. It was something Jared and his men would wear, only this man didn't appear to have any padded armor or weapons.

My eyes followed his shaking, bloody hands to an arrow sticking out of his stomach. He swallowed hard again, and dark blood gushed out of the puncture wound when he cleared his throat for a second time.

"He needs help," Dax said urgently.

"We don't even know who he is," Sadie said. "He could be the enemy."

Every breath he inhaled seemed like a difficult task, and I felt terrible for the man.

Don't feel bad, I told myself. Jared might have sent him out to kill you and everyone in Ortus.

I frowned at the thought.

"Who are you?" I shouted, jabbing my spear toward his face.

He flinched backward and released the arrow from his grip. It wiggled from side to side as he tried to crawl backward.

"P-p-please," he begged again. "I-I-I'm Samesh. I'm... I'm not even armed. Not anymore."

"Anymore," I repeated. "What did you have before?"

He stared at me, his honey-brown eyes making me think he was afraid to tell me.

I clenched my jaw, waiting.

"An M249 SAW," he said.

I raised an eyebrow, having no clue what he was talking about.

"Where the hell did you get a weapon like that?" James shouted.

"What is it?" I asked.

"An LMG," James said quickly, still

aggravated by the man's answer.

I must have still been giving James my confused look because he was quick to clarify. "A light machine gun."

A machine gun.

It made sense now.

"You're part of the crew that stole from my people when we were migrating," I said. "You stole horses, food, and one of our carts—"

Dax and Sadie stepped forward as if preparing to kick the man in the face.

"I-I'm sorry," the man said, cowering behind his raised arm. "It's what we do... it's how we survive."

"By stealing from others?" Dax growled.

He looked at her like the answer was obvious. "We have to. We don't have many people." Stopping, he looked away.

"Finish talking," I said.

He shook his head. "Nestor would kill me."

"Nestor?" I asked. "Is that your leader?"

Samesh didn't respond.

Whoever this Nestor was, Samesh was more afraid of him than he was of dying.

"Don't you want to live?" I asked.

Samesh stared at his bloody hands as if inspecting them for the last time. "It's too late for me. An injured man is useless to Nestor."

"You wouldn't be useless to us," I said.

Sadie nudged me in the side. "What are you doing?" she hissed.

Ignoring her, I kept talking to Samesh. "Why are you protecting a man who is leaving you for dead? If you tell us what we need to know about Nestor and his people, we'll take you to our doctors."

Samesh didn't look convinced, probably because Dax, Sadie, and James seemed to think I'd gone crazy. They tried to argue with me, but I told them to stay out of it.

"I stole from you," Samesh said. He paused, coughed up some blood, and then winced in pain. "Why would you help me live?"

I lowered my spear. "Because everyone deserves a second chance."

He stared at me for what felt like an eternity until he finally nodded. "If you can help me, I'll tell you everything you want to know."

"Come on," I said to the others. "Help me out."

Together, we picked up the man as he cried out in agony. It looked excruciating for him, but the sooner we got him to Ortus, the sooner we'd learn all about Nestor and his heavily armed men.

"On here," I said, pointing at Sadie's double saddle. Then, I turned to Dax. "Can you take him back?"

She nodded.

"This leaves us one horse short," Sadie said.

"We can take turns walking," I said. "Right

now, the only thing that matters is getting this man to Ortus."

Grunting, the four of us raised him onto the double-saddled horse.

Dax climbed in front of him, nearly knocking him over in the process.

"What happened to you, anyway?" she asked. "Who did this?"

Barely conscious now, Samesh said, "I-I-I don't know. Savages. In the trees. There were so many of them. Like a whole army."

Dax strapped his hands to the leather handle on the saddle, securing him in place while he swayed from side to side. Would he even manage to stay seated on the saddle? Or would he fall off?

Dax tugged hard one last time, binding his wrists together. "And these savages," she continued, "were they wearing wooden masks?"

Samesh rocked back again, but his head landed on Dax's shoulder when he came forward again.

"Did he just pass out?" she asked, looking down at us.

I rushed next to them, looking up at Samesh.

"Hey," Dax said, tapping the side of his head. "Get off me."

"Dax," I said.

"Get off me!" she kept saying. "Sit up

straight!"

"Dax!" I shouted.

She stopped smacking the man and stared at me.

I didn't have to say anything for her to realize what was happening.

With her hands, Dax pushed Samesh upright. His head bobbled a few times until he stopped moving entirely. His brown eyes were open, but he wasn't looking at anything.

CHAPTER 12

Dax jumped off her horse as if being attacked by a swarm of bees.

"Is he—"

"Dead," Sadie said coldly. "So much for getting information out of him."

I stared at his lifeless face, feeling sick to my stomach. Although I'd seen countless dead bodies over the last few weeks, it wasn't something I was numb to.

"Well, we did find out that there aren't many of them," James said.

Everyone went quiet, staring at the dead man.

"Let's get him off," I said.

Just like we'd struggled to get him up onto the horse, we struggled to get him down. Once we succeeded, we dragged his limp body to the forest's edge.

Even though he'd once been our enemy and stolen from us, leaving his body out in the open for animals to tear into didn't feel right.

It felt... disrespectful. And wrong. I had to do something.

If Grandma were here, she'd have told me that regardless of his past and his bad choices, he was still a human being.

"Help me out," I said, reaching for the rope in Dax's hands.

She looked confused but followed me anyway.

I wrapped the rope around his legs and formed several knots.

"What're you doing?" Sadie asked.

"Bringing him with us," I said, grunting to tighten the last knot.

"What? Why?" she said. "He's dead, Silver."

I stood up quickly and wiped my hands on my pants. "I know that. But he doesn't deserve to lie here and have his eyes pecked out by birds."

"Doesn't he?" she said. "Not long ago, he held us at gunpoint."

I shrugged. "Yeah, I know that. I'm not happy about it, but they didn't hurt any of us. They were probably desperate. The guy had parents at one point, and he might even have kids."

No one said anything, likely thinking I'd lost my mind. Either that or they simply didn't understand how I could put so much thought into a stranger's life—the life of an enemy.

Why was I going out of my way to dispose

of a body when I didn't even know the guy?

Because it was the right thing to do.

I fastened the other end of the rope to the back of my saddle, then climbed on.

"Silver," Dax said, "this is—"

"No one's perfect," I broke in. "People make choices based on their circumstances and their survival instincts. I don't know why you're all looking at me like that when we're about to steal a solar panel from Fort Denton. It's going to have an impact on the people who live there, but we're doing it anyway, right? Why? Because we need it. So stop looking at me like I'm crazy for wanting to give this guy a half-decent send-off to the afterlife."

No one said anything.

"Come on," I said, gently squeezing my horse's sides. "Nightfall's coming, and we need to set up camp."

We rode in silence with Samesh dragging through the grass behind me. Dax kept glancing down at him like she was grossed out.

"He's getting paler by the second," she said.

I didn't respond.

"I'm sorry about earlier," she said.

I looked at her sideways, waiting.

"For judging you," she said. "You know… about the whole body disposal thing."

Silent, I stared ahead at Sadie and James, who swayed gently on their horse. They were quiet, too, likely listening to Dax's apology.

"I think you have a huge heart, Silver," Dax said.

Still, I didn't respond. What did she want me to say? Did she expect me to thank her? I didn't want to receive a compliment for the choice I'd made. That wasn't why I'd done it.

"Sometimes, I worry that your heart will get you killed," she finally said.

I turned to look at her big brown—almost black—eyes. Her thick brows were slanted above them like she felt sorry for me.

"I know how to think with my heart *and* my head, Dax," I said, a bit more aggressively than I'd intended.

She parted her lips to say more, but I cut her off. "It doesn't inconvenience me to drag him to the river. It took a few minutes to tie him up. I wouldn't have done something like that if we were under attack."

"I didn't mean—"

"If we all start thinking about only ourselves," I said, "we'll end up like the Elites—heartless and self-serving. Maybe if more people took the time to realize that we're all in this together, we'd live in a better world. Everyone keeps acting like it's us against them, always. I'm sick of it. I don't understand why we can't just unite and live without conflict."

I breathed out hard through flared nostrils.

Dax didn't say anything more, and it was probably for the best.

After my outburst, I sat in silence, trying to understand where my anger was coming from.

And then it hit me.

After being tossed from the train and saved by Penelope, she'd given me hope. She'd made me feel safe and led me to believe that a happy life wasn't some far-fetched idea available only in Olympus and available only to those who won a lottery.

Even that—the lottery—had been a lie.

I didn't know what to believe anymore.

I'd always hoped that life outside of Lutum would be different... that I could live freely without violence and chaos. But ever since leaving Lutum, I'd seen more violence than inside Lutum's walls. I'd witnessed hundreds of deaths, limbs slashed off, throats slit, and arrows and bullets fired into countless bodies.

Why did humans hate each other so much?

Why couldn't we live peacefully?

I thought of the Woodfaces and how they'd come after me. Then, of Jared and his cruel ways. I thought of the men with their machine guns and how they'd stolen from us. I even thought back to Krampus, the chubby little man who'd shown up in Lockridge to take from Ari and her people.

This wasn't the world I wanted to live in.

My throat swelled, but I held back my tears.

If Grandma were with me, she'd tell me to hold on and that things would get better.

She always knew what to say.

"Why did they take them away, Grandma?" I asked, looking into her bright, gray-green eyes.

She ran a wrinkled thumb across my eyebrow, then my cheek. "We live in a cold world, sweetheart. Things can seem cruel and unfair, but I promise you that everything always works out in the end."

It was hard to imagine that things would *work out* after seeing a man and his newborn baby dragged away from his wife. I hadn't seen the argument, but he'd spoken back to a Defender, and it had caused a fight.

What about his wife? She'd given birth only a few days before; now, her husband and child were gone. Maybe forever. She threw herself in the mud, crying hysterically. She'd had a child without permission... and this was what happened when women birthed children without being granted a license by the Elites. The man and child were both taken, and no one knew where.

"But it's wrong," I said, my throat swelling. "They weren't bothering anyone. What's so dangerous about having a child?"

Grandma offered me a sad smile—a look that made me think she wanted to reach inside me and take away all the hurt.

"It is *wrong*," she said, poking my chest with her short finger. "But just because others do things that are wrong, it should never stop us from doing what's right."

"How do I know what's right?" I asked. "Wouldn't the right thing have been to help the man?"

Grandma sighed. "Yes, you're right," she said. "But like I said, this world is cruel and unfair. Sometimes doing the right thing puts you in more trouble, and you have to learn to do what's right at the right time."

My head spun with so many *rights* being thrown around.

"Listen to this," Grandma said, poking my chest again, right over my heart. Then, she tapped my temple. "But never forget to use this, too."

Smirking, I slapped her hand away, and she pulled me in for a hug.

"Silver?"

I was pulled out of my memory.

Up ahead, the sky was orange and pink, reminding me that there was still beauty in the world, and all we had to do was appreciate it.

Sadie and James were entering the forest, and James turned in his seat to look at me.

"Silver?"

When our eyes locked, he said, "We have to set up camp. Fort Denton is about a mile that way. Once the sun goes down, we can get the panel and come back here."

Without a word, I nodded and followed them into the dark forest.

CHAPTER 13

James unclipped the forest green bag from one of the saddles and brought it to the clearing we'd found. It wasn't a large space, but it was large enough to set up some blankets for a good night's sleep.

He unzipped the bag and pulled out what seemed like a lantern.

I observed him as he flipped it upside down and pressed something.

Suddenly, the lantern lit up.

"Let's use this sparingly," he said. "Batteries last about twelve hours. Once we come back, we should turn it off."

Batteries, I thought, staring at the flickering light. It looked so real, but I knew it wasn't. I'd seen this fake fire in Elias's room in the bunker. He'd even pointed at a fireplace that also made fake fire. It was both impressive and confusing.

Despite reading about them in many books, I had difficulty grasping the concept of batteries. As far as I understood, they stored energy. But I didn't understand where the energy came from.

James pulled out a few more things, such as rope, some sort of metal hook, and a bottle of water. Then, he pulled a gun out from his belt, inspected it, and put it back into its holster.

"You better not use that," Sadie said.

James froze, his hand hovering over the holster. "What? My gun?"

"Yeah," she said. "If that thing goes off, they'll come looking for us."

Hesitating, James reached into his holster and pulled it out. "You're right. Here. You keep it."

Before he could hand it to Sadie, Dax jumped in and snatched it. "I can handle this better. Mia snuck me into the range a few times."

She looked so excited holding the metal weapon that it was impossible not to smile.

Sadie pulled out two blankets from the bag and laid them on the ground next to the bright lantern. She sat down and let out a long breath. "Any food in there?"

James stuck his head in the back. "Yeah. A few granola bars that Arahm made." He reached inside, pulled out a wooden box, and handed it to Sadie.

Dax jumped next to her to peek inside.

"Are those raisins?" Dax asked.

"No, dead flies," Sadie said.

Dax pulled her face back so far that a roll formed under her chiseled jaw. "What? That's disgust—"

Sadie smirked. "They're raisins."

Dax smacked Sadie's shoulder, but when Sadie's eyes went big, she retreated. Although Dax was stronger and tougher-looking than Sadie, Sadie had a way of making people cower with her cold blue eyes.

"Got your crossbow?" Sadie asked.

I nodded, untying it from my saddle.

The horses stood quietly, munching on grass and flowers near tree roots. I gave one of them a gentle tap on the butt to thank them for bringing us all this way.

"We'll be back soon," I said to Sadie and Dax.

As we started walking away, Sadie whistled.

When we turned to look at her, she gave James a threatening look. "You'd better have her back in one piece."

James wrapped an arm around me playfully. "Don't worry. We'll be fine."

I hoped he was right.

The last thing we needed right now was another attack or another war.

"You sure this'll be easy?" I whispered.

He led me through the dark forest with that strange black stick he held lighting the way. "Piece of cake."

CHAPTER 14

We spent the next ten minutes arguing about what he'd just said: *piece of cake.*

"It doesn't make sense," I said. "How is that supposed to mean *easy*? Why not say *easy*? Or *simple*?"

"It's a saying, Silver," he said. "It's only a saying... As in, something people say instead of saying it's easy."

"But why?" I asked. "Why do people complicate English like that?"

He sighed and shook his head. Although I couldn't see his face in the darkness, I got the impression he was laughing at me.

"It keeps things interesting, I don't know," he said, his feet crunching several twigs. "My mom used to say that to me all the time."

I stopped walking. I'd never heard James talk about either of his parents.

"Your mom," I said.

He stopped and pointed his light toward

me.

"What about her?" he asked.

I raised my arm to shield my eyes, and he immediately lowered the light. "You never talk about her. Is she alive?" I asked.

When he went quiet, I wondered if my question had been rude.

"No," he said, matter-of-factly. "Neither is my dad, in case you're wondering."

"What happened?" I asked.

He didn't seem too bothered talking about it. I wondered how long it had been since he'd lost his parents.

"What happens to most people's parents, I guess," he said. "Illness. It's not like we had a bunch of medication to save everyone inside Fort Denton. I heard that back in the day, hospitals saved a lot of lives. Maybe if we lived back then, things would be different."

I thought of Lyla and Lyson and how they, too, had lost their parents. Even Sadie had no parents.

"It's stupid, actually," he said. "My mom cut her ankle on a stone while gardening, and it got infected. My dad caught the flu five years ago. It was a nasty one that killed sixty-three people in the bunker."

"Oh... I'm so sorry," I said.

"Don't be," he said. "It's life, and we're all one tiny infection away from death. That's how I see it. That's why it's important to live every day like it's your last."

Live every day like it's your last, I thought.

I'd never heard that before, but I liked it.

"See that?" James said, pointing ahead. When I couldn't tell what he was pointing at, he aimed his stick of light upward a bit. "I don't want to point my light directly on the courtyard wall if someone's watching," he added. "But that right there is where the walls start."

To the left of us was nothing but an open field. For miles, the tall grass looked white beneath the full moon, and it was something I'd always found beautiful. In Lutum, I'd stick my head out the window for hours, admiring a full moon as often as possible.

"They say people act cuckoo on a full moon," James said.

"Cuckoo?" I asked.

What was he talking about?

"Like, crazy," he said. "Weird. Odd. Unusual."

"Does this have anything to do with—" I paused, trying to remember the word. "Astrology?"

He shrugged. "I guess so."

Mother had ripped the only book I'd ever read on astrology from my hands when she found me reading it under my blanket. She'd said that astrology was worse than religion and that I should stay away from it.

Now that my world had been turned upside down and I no longer knew what to believe, I'd promised to visit Ortus's underground library—if I ever got back to Ortus—and locate a book on astrology.

"You aren't going to turn into a werewolf, are you?" he asked.

"A what?" I said.

He flashed his light at me, but only for a second, like he was trying to gauge whether I was joking.

"Your people didn't share many stories where you're from, did they?" he asked.

I shook my head, though I realized he couldn't see me.

"No," I said plainly. "We weren't allowed to. At least not out in the open."

His feet crunched more twigs and leaves, and he sighed. "Maybe it's for the best. Here I am, wondering if there's some wolf monster lurking nearby, waiting to eat us both alive—"

"What?" I blurted. "Wolf monster?"

I'd seen a wolf for the first time before Penelope died. I'd seen several of them. I couldn't imagine what a wolf *monster* looked like. It sounded terrifying.

"Never mind," he said. "Let's focus on the mission."

I swallowed hard, gripping my crossbow a bit tighter than necessary.

Around us, everything was black.

The only light we had was the circular white glow projected by James' black metal stick.

"What is that?" I asked.

He searched the dark forest with the light. "What?"

"No, that—" I pointed at the stick in his hand, but before he noticed I was pointing, he aimed it at me, blinding me again.

"Oh, sorry, this—" He twirled it around a few times, and the light lit up the tree branches overhead. They looked like a bunch of giant spider legs preparing to crush us.

"It's called a flashlight," he said. "You know, because it flashes light."

He pointed it in all directions as if trying to make his point.

"Does it also work with... batteries?" I asked.

"Exactly," he said. "It's like the lantern I pulled out earlier, only this one has a brighter bulb, and the shape of the glass is made to project light far away."

When I didn't say anything, he offered it to me. "Want to try?"

I couldn't say no. I was too curious to see what it felt like to hold artificial light.

The weight of it was heavier than I had expected. I twirled it around in my palms a few times, the rough texture making my skin itch.

"You just aim where you want to see, and it

lights it up for you."

Smiling, I aimed it right in James's face. He winced and threw his hands up in the air.

"Hey!" he said.

I laughed. "That's for all the other times."

I lowered the light to his chest when he didn't laugh back, and it seemed to bounce off his body and light us both up.

"You okay?" I asked.

Frowning, he pinched the bridge of his nose and blinked hard a few times. He didn't look okay.

"Yeah," he said, his voice strange. "Sorry. I have a condition with my eyes. Makes me extremely sensitive to light."

"Oh, I'm sorry—"

He waved a hand in the air. "It's not your fault. You didn't know."

I spotted the red-framed sunglasses on his head. "Is that why you always wear those?"

He nodded, still squinting as if trying to force the pain out of his eyes.

"Light gives me nasty migraines," he said.

"Those are like headaches, right?"

He scoffed. "Sure, like headaches. But way worse."

"I... I'm sorry."

"You didn't know," he said. He reached for the flashlight and turned it off. "We should continue in the dark anyway. If they see the light in the forest, it's game over."

I wasn't sure why he was referring to our mission as a *game*, but I didn't want to bother him with more questions.

"Come on, follow me," he said, reaching for my hand.

I wasn't sure how he knew where to walk, but I imagined that since he avoided light most of the time, maybe his eyes worked better in the dark.

CHAPTER 15

T his is it," he whispered. "The eastern wall."

The overhead moon and stars shined down on the courtyard's wall, revealing the massive gates we'd escaped from only yesterday. They were sealed shut, and no Woodface bodies were in sight.

"Over there is where the panel is," he whispered. "Come on."

We walked past the gates and toward the very end of the courtyard, where the stone wall formed a sharp corner.

"All I have to do is get up there," he said.

With hands on his hips, he spun around a few times, searching the sky above us.

"What about that tree?" I asked, pointing at the nearest one.

It looked thick enough to handle plenty of weight with its massive branches that reached out like pleading arms. Maybe if he climbed high enough, he'd make the jump to the top of the wall.

It was still a risk, though.

"That's what I was thinking," he said.

I tried calculating the distance between the nearest branch, but I'd never been any good at measuring anything. Grandma had taught me that one foot, in measurements, was about two hands' worth, or at least, my hands. The Defenders had never allowed us to use *measuring tape* to build our garden beds.

"You look worried," James said.

"Well, I am," I admitted. "Can you even make that jump?"

He shook his head. "No way. That's like ten feet, and the tip of the branch would crack if I put all my weight on it."

The way he spoke told me he wasn't concerned about not being able to make the jump. So, what else did he have planned?

Without a word, he unwrapped a long rope from around his waist. Then, from a small bag around his shoulder, he plucked a metallic claw I'd seen Maz pack for us earlier. I'd thought it was a weapon at the time, but now, I wasn't so sure.

I watched curiously as James tied one end of his rope around this mysterious claw.

"It's a grappling hook," he said, twirling the shiny metal tool.

The moonlight reflected off its sharp hooks—all three of them.

It reminded me of a flower, only it looked far deadlier with its solid stem and sharp petals.

James poked one of the sharp points with his index finger when I didn't say anything. "See these? They're meant to catch on to something. If I can get a good grip on the other side, I can climb up the rest of the wall."

Now, it made sense.

He had planned to climb the tree and toss that *grappling hook* over for the rest of the climb.

"You sure it'll hold?" I asked.

"As long as I can catch it on something solid," he said. "Hopefully, I don't catch the panel."

I couldn't tell if he was trying to be funny, so I didn't respond.

"You keep an eye out," he said. "If you see anything, whistle."

"Whistle?" I said.

He froze, holding on to his sharp hook. "Yeah... whistle. Can't you whistle?"

I tightened my lips and sucked in, releasing a pathetic, wavering sound.

"Why do you suck in?" he said. "Blow out when you whistle."

I tried to blow out with tight lips, but no whistle came. I must have been making a stupid face; he slapped the air as if to say, "Don't worry about it," and wrapped the rope around his arm. "I'll be back, and tomorrow, I'm teaching you how to whistle."

He disappeared into the forest.

Every few seconds, a faint grunting noise escaped his lungs. As he climbed, his sounds became fainter. I craned my neck, hoping to spot him, but all I saw were shaking branches and leaves falling to the ground.

It wasn't until he emerged from one of the branches that I spotted his dark silhouette.

He might have given me a thumbs-up, but I couldn't be sure.

I felt sick to my stomach watching him slide across the tree branch on his belly, little by little. He was so high up that I worried he'd die if he fell off. Either that or break several bones, making it impossible to take him back to Ortus without him suffering excruciating pain.

I shook those thoughts away.

Right now, all that mattered was that he make it over that wall and grab the solar panel without getting caught.

We hadn't talked about how long it would take him to get it, so I hoped he knew what he was doing.

Halfway across the branch, the wood slanted under his weight. He pulled out his grapple and started swinging it above his head.

I tensed when he threw it toward the wall. The metal slammed into the stone wall and bounced off with a scraping sound.

He'd missed.

He tried again, and it wasn't until his third attempt that the hook landed over the wall. He pulled on the rope until it became tight, then pulled on it some more.

I tried to remember what the inside the courtyard looked like, and I hoped he'd caught on to something sturdy, like the wooden beam of a stable.

Slowly, he stood, and the branch seemed to bend even more.

If he walked any farther, I was afraid the wood might snap.

He tugged on the rope as if trying to reassure himself that it would hold. After several tugs, he leaned back and let himself fall off the branch.

My stomach sank as he swung through the air, landing with his feet flat against the exterior wall.

Using his arms and legs, he started climbing the rope.

Thankfully, there wasn't much to climb, but watching him go up made me nauseous.

When he reached the top, he swung one leg over, gave me a black silhouetted thumbs-up, and disappeared behind the wall.

My eyes shot in every direction—toward the main gates, the forest, the field.

How long would this take?

I swallowed hard, and my heart pounded

against my ribs.

I felt helpless standing there, waiting.

If he got caught, I couldn't help him; I didn't have a grappling hook, and even if I did, I wouldn't know how to use it. The main gates were sealed shut and couldn't be opened from the outside.

I started pacing, telling myself that everything would be fine.

It was nighttime.

It wasn't like anyone patrolled the courtyard at night. Why would they? Everyone was sealed inside the bunker, entirely protected.

Besides, Jared had lost half the bunker's citizens. They didn't have enough people to assign as night guards.

Right?

My mouth became dry as I walked back and forth.

Suddenly, a rustling sound caught my attention. Although tempted to use James's flashlight, I didn't. The last thing we needed was for *me* to ruin this entire mission.

I squinted into the forest's darkness, my crossbow aimed at the sound.

With my finger hovering over the trigger button, I waited.

If someone was planning to attack, I'd shoot first.

I wondered if Dax or Sadie had followed us

here. As much as I wanted to call out, I couldn't. Staying quiet was the only way we'd escape this place with the solar panel in our hands.

So I waited until suddenly, another sound caught my attention—leaves crunching.

I shifted my aim to the right, only to find two big green eyes glowing in the dark. They stared at me, almost as if waiting to see whether or not I'd make the first move.

They weren't big enough to belong to a dangerous animal like a wolf.

But they were bigger than any green eyes I'd seen exploring our garden beds in Lutum.

What was that thing?

At once, the eyes disappeared and the creature scampered away, its little claws digging into tree bark.

Closing my eyes, I let out a long breath.

At the same time, a bright light caught my attention.

I snapped my head sideways to spot white light spilling out inside the courtyard. Only seconds ago, everything had been pitch black. Why were the lights on? Had James been spotted? I raced toward the corner of the wall, hoping to see James climbing back over to my side.

He wasn't there.

Where was he?

Suddenly, grunting echoed from the other side.

James, I wanted to shout.
They'd caught him.
It was over.

CHAPTER 16

Without warning, a dark leg came swinging over the courtyard's stone wall.

The light from inside the courtyard lit up half of James's face. But the moment he swung over completely, he became nothing more than a dark figure again. His hair, a complete mess, looked like a wild animal's nest. Although I couldn't see his features on this side of the wall, he waved at me in a panic.

"Come here!" he hissed. "You need to catch this."

He held the rope tightly, his body bouncing all over the place. Then, he lost some grip and slid down the wall several feet.

"I can't... I can't hold—"

Suddenly, something fell out from underneath his arm.

I rushed toward him and stuck my arms out, preparing myself to catch the unknown.

It didn't land softly. Something sharp

suddenly sliced my cheek open, and another hard piece slammed against my chin. The rest of the weight crashed into my chest. I squinted in pain and took several steps back, the impact knocking me off-balance.

James walked backward down the wall just as I fell to the ground, still carefully holding on to what I could only assume was the solar panel.

"Shit, shit, shit." It sounded like he was in pain.

When he was close enough to the ground, he jumped backward, landing softly in the grass, then shook his hands wildly in the air.

"Ah, that burns," he said, clenching his fists.

I reached for my cheek, feeling warm blood trickle toward my jaw and down my neck.

"You okay?" he asked. "Never mind, we have to go."

He snatched the solar panel out of my hands and helped me up.

"Come on!"

I ran after him, my heart pounding.

Were they coming after us? Were the gates about to open? What was going on?

"James!" I hissed behind him.

I stumbled a few times, my feet catching on to tree roots. Yet, I somehow managed to stay on my feet. Several branches whipped me in the face, but all I could do was keep running.

It wasn't until I'd chased after James for a

few minutes that he stopped.

Panting, he slumped forward, breathing heavily.

"What happened?" I asked. "What's going on?"

Without responding, he started patting my pockets until he found the flashlight. He pulled it out, turned it on, and aimed it at the shiny black rectangle in his arms. It was an awkward size—small enough to be carried by a person but too big to be held with only one arm.

It was thick and looked like it was made of metal and glass.

"A few scratches, but it looks good," he said.

Without warning, he aimed his light at my face, and I shut my eyes.

"Sorry about that," he said. "I thought I had more time. I never meant to make you catch it."

I licked blood off my lips but didn't respond.

"I must have triggered something in the wiring when I disconnected the panel. All the lights turned on," he said.

"Are you sure you did that? Maybe they saw you."

"Pretty sure it was me," he said. "But it doesn't matter. If anyone notices the lights on, they'll inspect and see the grapple hook. I couldn't get it out."

"And the missing solar panel," I added.

He looked down at the panel as if only now remembering that he'd stolen it. "Right, that too."

After a pause, he said, "Either way, we need to get back to camp and stay quiet. It's only a matter of time before they come looking for their thief."

I followed James back to our camp, and when we got there, both Dax and Sadie let out huge sighs of relief.

"We were worried," Sadie said. Then, spotting the damage the panel had caused to my face, she rushed toward me. "What happened to you?"

I shook my head as if to say, *It's not a big deal.*

Her hateful gaze turned on James. "I told you to bring her back—"

"It's not his fault," I said. "We had to bring the panel down fast, so I caught it."

Before she could argue, I said, "Let's turn off the lantern and get some rest. At dawn, we need to get across the river."

CHAPTER 17

By morning, I felt as though I'd only slept an hour.

I probably had.

The four of us had taken turns keeping watch of the forest in case Jared and his men came out looking for us. Fortunately, that didn't happen. Aside from little creatures roaming the tree branches, the night had remained mostly quiet.

"Time to go," I grumbled, my eyelids feeling heavier than ever.

Dax grumbled something and rolled over, not wanting to get off her thin blanket.

"Once this is over, we can go back to Ortus and sleep," I said.

I hesitated, remembering what I'd told the people of Ortus—I wasn't coming back. Sadie must have remembered this, too. She gave me a scowl that told me she wasn't impressed with my lie.

Deep down, I hadn't meant for it to be a lie.

I wanted to go back to Ortus, but only once it was safe to do so without the Elites hunting me down.

I picked up my crossbow and walked over to my horse, petting her soft muzzle. She looked as tired as I felt, lying in the dirt with the rest of the horses. Behind her was Samesh's body. I did my best not to look at his colorless face and hollow eyes.

"We're almost done," I told her.

Although the horse didn't make any sound, I got the feeling she understood me. Those big brown eyes made me feel something special. Part of me wanted to hug her neck, but I wasn't yet *that* comfortable around horses and wasn't sure how she'd react.

"How do we get them up?" I asked.

Sadie smiled and slowly rose to her feet. She made a clicking sound with her mouth and started pulling at their reins one by one.

I was surprised by how quickly they shot upright, their heavy hooves stomping on the ground.

Within minutes, we packed our bag and the solar panel and continued our path through the field toward the broken bridge.

"Wait," I said, suddenly realizing something.

Everyone stopped to look at me.

"We should stay in the forest," I said. "If we keep going down this path, we'll be exposed."

Trees didn't surround the broken bridge—it was completely open. To make matters worse, the bunker wasn't all that far, either. I remembered the day we arrived there and how Elias had opened up the bunker not too far away.

It was all over if Jared and his men decided to come out with guns.

"What are you suggesting?" James asked. "I was planning on using the concrete from the bridge to hold the rope for us, you know, when we cross over. I won't make you swim, don't worry. I'll swim over and tie the other end—"

"What's wrong with using tree trunks for that?" I asked.

He smirked at me. "All right. Back into the forest, it is."

We barely made it into the forest when the horses started acting irritated. Not only that, but Samesh's body got stuck on a large root.

"The horses can't walk through here," Sadie pointed out. "And we need to do something about him—"

She pointed at Samesh, looking disturbed. I didn't blame her. I was beginning to feel uncomfortable about dragging a dead body around. I had hoped we would reach the river easily and that I could dump his body in the water, but things were only becoming more and more difficult.

And with how thick the forest was, Sadie

was right—we couldn't travel with the horses.

"Let's tie them up," Sadie said, jumping off her horse.

She helped James down, which I could tell made him uncomfortable.

"I'm good," he said as he landed with a thud. He then went on to pat dust off his chest and pants.

Poor James. He looked embarrassed, and I supposed he was. James was very good at driving the rover, but when it came to horseback riding, he knew nothing about it. And it was obvious that James took pride in being good at driving.

Sadie tied the horses to nearby trees and rubbed each one between the eyes as if saying goodbye.

"We'll be back," she whispered.

Then, she gave me a stern look. "We need to do something about him. He'll attract predators and put the horses at risk—"

"Fine," I said, waving a hand in the air.

I couldn't help but feel disappointed as Sadie and Dax untied his ankles and dragged him farther out into the forest.

It's not your problem, I told myself. At least you tried.

James grabbed our bag, and when Dax returned, she held on to the solar panel with her long arms.

"Where'd you put him?" I asked.

Sadie wiped her hands on her thighs. "Doesn't matter."

I supposed it didn't.

I parted my lips, prepared to ask if the horses would be okay on their own, when Dax's horse started munching on leaves overhead. It wasn't long before the others followed.

We crossed the forest until we approached the fast-moving river. A breeze swept through the air, bringing with it little droplets of water that made my mouth water. But as we got closer, the water looked darker and the current more aggressive.

The sight of it made my stomach feel funny.

Suddenly, I remembered being pulled by the current, unable to swim to the side. The pull had been so strong, like mighty, invisible arms pulling me down. My mouth went dry, and I swallowed hard. The last thing I wanted was to relive something like that.

"Don't worry," James said as if reading my mind. "You won't have to swim across this time. I have a better plan."

I hoped he was right. The idea of trying to swim across again made me want to abandon this mission altogether. I wasn't so sure I'd survive this time.

"You swam this?" Sadie asked, raising her eyebrows.

She pointed at the water, but I couldn't respond. All I could focus on was the loud humming sound from the water.

I didn't remember the water being so loud; I'd been too focused on keeping my head above it... on trying to survive.

Sadie suddenly poked my shoulder, and I caught her stare.

She didn't ask me the same question twice. Instead, she made her eyebrows go up even higher on her forehead.

James cleared his throat, likely sensing how uncomfortable I was reliving the memory.

"She did her best," he said. "We helped her by throwing in a rope."

I ignored Sadie's glare and forced a smile at James.

Although he wasn't wrong, that wasn't the whole story. I was glad he left out the part about me almost drowning and being carried away forever. Sadie didn't need to hear that. She already worried about me enough as it was.

James dropped his dark green bag onto the forest floor and pulled out a rope.

I stood on the tips of my toes, trying to see inside the bag.

How many ropes had Maz packed for us? We'd lost one last night after James climbed the courtyard wall.

"This one should work." James raised the rope to eye level, the rest falling to the ground and forming circles.

No one said anything as he wrapped one end of the rope around the base of a slanted tree. He tugged hard once, twice, and then three times to ensure his knot was secure.

"That'll hold," he said, more to himself than anyone else.

Then, he wrapped the other end around his torso and walked straight up to the edge of the forest, where a significant drop led into the river. Was he planning on jumping in?

"Wait!" I said. "What are you doing? What's the plan?"

James smirked at me the way he'd done before racing the rover out of the underground parking lot. Now that he wasn't riding a horse, his confidence was back.

"Have some faith," he said, slipping his sunglasses into his front pocket.

Without warning, he dropped headfirst into the river, and my heart clenched.

I ran to the edge of the drop, causing dirt and little pebbles to fall into the river.

A firm hand suddenly grabbed the back of my shirt, pulling me back a few steps.

"Easy," Dax said. "The guy knows what he's doing."

Did he, though? Why couldn't I see him? I stared into the brown water, my heart pounding. Why wasn't he resurfacing? Then, I remembered what he'd told me last time. It was normal to be pulled sideways by the current, which meant he wouldn't resurface where he'd jumped in.

I looked farther ahead and more to the left, waiting.

"Come on," I mumbled.

Suddenly, a blond head popped out of the water, and James gasped for air.

It looked like he was smiling.

Was he enjoying this?

He waved at us with a cheesy grin, then gave me a thumbs-up as the water pulled him.

I glanced down at the rope near my feet.

There was still plenty left, which reassured me. If the current took him for some reason, the rope would prevent him from being swept too far away.

Sadie pressed a gentle hand on my shoulder. "See? He's fine."

I let out a breath, realizing I'd been holding it in.

I watched as James swam hard toward the other side. From where I stood, it didn't look like he was making any progress. It seemed like the river didn't want him to reach the other side.

But finally, he did.

The other side was similar to ours—a dirt cliff. But it wasn't as high up, and James had no trouble climbing it. Grabbing tree roots that stuck out of the dirt wall, he pulled himself onto the surface and sat for a moment, catching his breath.

He gave us another wave as if to say, *All good!* and got to his feet.

From where I stood, his hair looked brown and his clothes three shades darker. He ran a hand through his wet hair, combing out the water, then plucked his sunglasses from his pocket and slipped them on.

Next, he went over to a tree and pulled at the loose rope in the river. The rope began to unwind at our feet quickly, and over the river, it tightened until it formed a straight line.

Once the rope was snug, James fastened a knot around a tree and tugged several more times.

He waved once more and gestured with a thumbs-up. "Come on!"

I looked over at Sadie, then Dax, and swallowed hard. How was this rope supposed to get us across? Was I supposed to hang from it? I'd never done this before.

But before I could say or do anything, Dax smiled and said, "I'll go first."

CHAPTER 18

For some reason, watching Dax cross the rope upside down was even scarier than having watched James dive headfirst into the river.

Every time she wrapped her fingers around the slanted rope, I cringed, afraid she might slip and fall into the water.

And if she did, everything was over.

She'd fastened the solar panel to the rope ahead of her. It hung by a short piece of rope and a few sturdy knots. Every time Dax moved closer to James's side of the river, she pushed the panel by a few inches, moving it along with her.

The panel swayed side to side, reflecting the sunlight's bright yellow glow. What if the knot came undone? What if—

"Remind me to see Bhavna when we return to Ortus," Sadie said.

I didn't correct her on the *we* part. Although I wasn't planning on returning anytime soon, I hoped to one day. There was no use in correcting Sadie whenever she talked about us returning together.

But who was Bhavna, and what did she have to do with this?

Confused, I scrunched my nose, prepared to ask her what she was talking about.

"Breathe," she said.

It was only then that I realized I was holding my breath again. I let out a lungful of air and wiped my sweaty palms on my pants.

"Bhavna is Ortus's herbalist," she said.

Before I could even ask her what an herbalist was, she smirked. "Some people call her the village witch, but it's all in good fun. She knows everything there is to know about medicinal herbs and has some potent chamomile that might help with your anxiety."

I thought back to Asako and the panic attack she'd had. Was Sadie trying to tell me I could have one, too? Or that I was about to have one? The thought made my heart race.

"Anxiety?" I repeated.

She smiled sweetly at me. "It has many forms. And ever since the Woodfaces attacked us, you've been on edge. Even more than when I met you, which is saying a lot."

I wasn't even sure what being on edge meant, but I knew she was telling me I'd changed somehow. And not for the better... that I was somehow filled with anxiety. I didn't respond. I couldn't. The truth was, I was terrified every day, never knowing when someone else might attack us.

I never felt safe. Worse, I felt even more vulnerable than I had in Lutum.

The only time I'd felt somewhat normal was inside the bunker. But ever since we'd left, I was right back to feeling like prey.

"I know what chamomile is," I said. "Grandma used to make tea for my mom. We didn't have much of it in the garden, but she said it helped Mother with her nightmares."

Sadie looked like she was about to question me on Mother when suddenly, Dax let out a birdlike chirp. It wasn't something I'd expect from Dax's large, muscular body, and it was enough to pull my attention in.

With her legs wrapped firmly around the rope, she now hung upside down, the ends of her short brown hair hanging a few feet above the fast-moving water.

I didn't have to look twice to understand why she'd let go of the rope.

Against her chest was the solar panel—without any rope.

What had happened? Had the knot come undone?

"It broke!" Dax shouted, her body rocking back and forth.

Although tempted to tell Sadie, "You see? I was right to be worried," I kept my mouth shut.

Across the river, James paced back and forth between two trees, running his hands through his hair. He covered his mouth and lowered himself into a crouched position as if trying to get a better view. His brows rose above his shades, and he looked about as panicked as I felt.

Sadie froze but blurted, "It's okay… it's okay. If anyone's got this, it's Dax."

Her words didn't convince me; she looked about as scared as James and I, but Sadie wasn't the type to express how she felt. She'd lie through her teeth if it meant keeping the rest of us calm.

Dax squirmed like a fish out of water, trying to get a good grip on the panel. It was nauseating to watch. Despite how strong Dax was, it was apparent she was struggling to hold on to the solar panel. She slapped the shiny black thing a few times—a quick gesture to secure it against her body. When she finally managed to wrap a single arm around it, she pulled herself up and gripped the rope with her left hand.

Then, she started moving again with only one hand carrying her upper body.

Every inch of progress she made felt like a mile.

"Come on, come on," Sadie muttered.

When Dax made it to the other side, everyone breathed out at the same time.

James stretched his arm out, reaching for the panel before even offering Dax any help. She didn't seem bothered by this. If anything, she seemed to have the same idea in mind. She handed him the panel, then swayed upside down for a second before James came back to help her.

Grabbing the rope, she pulled herself toward the river's edge before awkwardly letting go. She nearly fell to the ground, but James caught her and helped her back up onto her feet.

"Your turn," Sadie said.

I wasn't sure if she was trying to be friendly or if she was afraid to go next after what had happened. Then again, knowing Sadie, she probably wanted to stay behind me in case something happened and I needed help.

She led me to the rope.

"You've got this," she said, tightening a knot on the short, stretchy rope James had used to secure our weapons, which was now around my waist.

I stared below at the fast-moving water, suddenly wondering if maybe this whole thing was a terrible idea. Maybe there was another way across.

"Stop thinking," she said. "Just act."

Just act, I thought. It was easier said than done.

I wiped my clammy hands against my pants

and gripped the rope. Sadie helped swing my legs up until I wrapped them around the rope, clutching on for dear life.

The second she let go of me, I hung there, the rope stretching with the weight of my body.

My heart raced, and I wondered if my palms would become too wet for me to hold on.

One wrong move...

"Unlike Dax, you don't have a panel to bring with you," she said. "Close your eyes and keep moving."

I closed my eyes, breathing hard. But surprisingly, this trick worked. Within seconds, I felt calmer, more at ease. As I moved down the rope, I kept my closed eyes aimed at the sky and listened only to Sadie's voice behind me as she shouted, "Almost there!"

For a moment, I forgot about the water's roar beneath me or the cold breeze sweeping upward, cooling my back.

Reach the other side, I told myself. That's all you have to do.

Up ahead, James's voice became clearer the closer I got.

"Almost there, Silver. That's it. All right." His voice was loud now. "I've got you. Come here."

I cracked my eyes open to find him upside down.

Then I remembered that I was the one upside down.

He reached forward, grabbed me under the arms, and pulled me off the rope.

"See?" he said, grinning. "Not so bad, was it?"

I forced a smile and rubbed at my pink palms.

James laughed and showed me his. They were red and blistered in the middle.

"From last night," he said, "when I came rushing down."

I must have made a face. James laughed again and closed his fists. "It'll heal."

We waited as Sadie made her way across. It was like she'd done this a hundred times over. It was probably her first time, but Sadie had a way of making everything look effortless. With a hardened face, she moved fast as if trying to beat the time we'd made—as if this was nothing more than a training drill in Ortus.

I hoped that one day, I'd have her confidence. Or, maybe it wasn't confidence at all and only an act. Either way, I admired her for it.

But then, something loud echoed all around us, and Sadie's serious features melted into a look of terror.

Gunshots.

Without warning, dirt exploded around my feet.

I threw an arm in front of my face as if it would somehow protect me.

I didn't even think to reach for my crossbow. Somehow, I knew there was no point. I wouldn't have the time to unfasten the knot around my abdomen, load a bolt, and locate our enemy.

Another gunshot went off, missing Sadie by a hair and ripping into the tree James had used to fasten the rope. It wasn't until the fourth shot was fired that one of the bullets tore through the rope's knot, breaking it instantly.

A loud snapping sound filled the forest.

Then, a sharp hissing noise followed, and the rope began to unwind from around the tree trunk.

I only caught a glimpse of Sadie's terrified face—huge blue eyes, a gaping mouth, and slanted brows that told me she knew she wouldn't make it across the river—before she disappeared entirely, falling straight into the river.

I lunged for the rope, landing flat on my stomach against a tree root. My elbows clashed with something sharp, but I ignored the pain.

Although the plan had been heroic—I'd wanted to grab the rope before it slipped away and off the cliff—everything happened too quickly.

My fingers didn't even come close to touching the broken rope.

I lay there in disbelief as the rest of the rope leading to the other side went slack and fell into the water. I followed it up the cliff, hoping to spot our attacker standing on the other side, when James grabbed me by the shirt and shouted, "Run!"

More bullets flew toward us, causing dirt to explode all around us.

So I did the only thing my survival instincts allowed me to do—I ran.

CHAPTER 19

Eventually, the bullets stopped, and we stood deeper inside the forest.

I spun around, my chest heaving. "Sadie!"

Dax slapped a hand over my mouth and, with button-shaped eyes, warned me to keep quiet.

"Did they get her?" I asked. I wanted to run back to the river. "Did they shoot her? Was she shot? Did anyone see?"

Both Dax and James shook their heads.

"Didn't see," Dax said.

Without thinking, I started running back toward our attackers, but Dax caught me in midair as I jumped over a branch.

"Don't be stupid," she said.

"We don't have time to go back for her," James said. "I'm betting those were Jared's men. They figured out we have the panel, and they're coming for us."

I breathed in hard to catch my breath. How could he stand there and worry about Jared's men and the panel when Sadie had fallen into the river? We had to get her back. We were running out of time. If she was injured, she wouldn't be able to swim—

"Let's move," James said.

I wanted to argue, but I knew James was right. My feelings for Sadie only blinded me, and I wanted to keep her safe above all else— even my own life.

So rather than freeze and overthink everything, I followed James and Dax. Maybe all we needed was to come up with a plan to save Sadie *and* not get killed.

"Where are we going?" I hissed.

"To the rover," James said.

The rover?

"Sadie needs our help!" I shouted.

Without looking back at me, James yelled, "Sadie could be dead, Silver! And if we don't get this rover, we're all dead!"

Hundreds of thoughts raced through my mind. How could he say that? Why couldn't we save Sadie first and then get the rover?

"He's right," Dax said, running next to me. Her words were choppy through her rapid breaths. "If they're onto us, it's only a matter of time before they figure out *why* we stole the panel, if they don't already know."

James placed his hands on his hips, looking more serious than ever.

"Sadie's a survivor," Dax added. "She'll know

to keep going upstream, away from danger."

I wanted to believe her, but what if Sadie had been shot? What if she was bleeding out in the water while we chased after the rover?

Then, I realized that if Sadie were here, she'd tell me to keep running and continue the mission.

So I did exactly that, fighting with myself to push her out of my mind.

When we reached the edge of the forest, near where the rover had been left, James stopped abruptly and threw his arms out as if to say, *Don't go any farther.*

Was the rover gone?

Ignoring him, I pushed one of his arms down and craned my neck to see up ahead.

The rover was there—completely intact. It sat near the river's edge with grass bits stuck to its metallic frame.

"It could be a trap," he said.

On the other side of the river were beams of wood piled on top of one another. Those hadn't been there before and certainly weren't part of the ramp we'd built—the ramp Jared had destroyed.

So what was all of that material? What was Jared planning?

"What is that?" I asked, pointing at the wood.

"Looks like they're preparing to build a bridge," James said. "They were probably planning on retrieving the rover that way."

I couldn't see anyone on the other side of the river. What if standing here talking about a potential trap was a waste of time? Time we didn't have.

"We should go now," I said.

James wasn't convinced. His features hardened while he inspected the other side. "They could be hiding."

"Or, they could be running," Dax said. "Running down the river, looking for us. We should act fast."

Although James stood quietly, I could tell he was thinking about every scenario imaginable. He sighed, then reached for his holstered gun.

I took a step back and immediately felt stupid.

It wasn't like James was going to hurt us. He was a good guy. Maybe it had to do with the fact that someone had just fired bullets at us.

"Here," he said, handing the gun to me.

I took another step back. "What? Why are you giving me that?"

"Because I need someone to cause a distraction if they are on the other side, waiting," he said.

I still didn't understand what he was saying.

He shook the gun in the air as if to say, *Go on, take it.*

I didn't.

Sighing, he said, "Look, it's very easy. I'm going to show you how to cock it and how to shoot. You don't need to know how to aim. All you need to do is shoot in their general direction, and they'll shift their focus to you."

Swallowing hard, I stared at the dirty metal. Why was it so intimidating? I hadn't been this afraid to hold a crossbow, which was also lethal.

Then, I thought of something. "Why can't I just fire my crossbow?"

James shook his head, my reflection shifting from one lens to the other in his glasses. "It's the loud sound we need."

Dax stepped in. "I can do it."

Not wanting to waste any more time, James placed the gun in her hand and nodded as if to thank her. At the same time, he grabbed the solar panel from her grip. Then, in a strange, almost crouched position, he started running toward the rover.

I waited, my heart pounding.

Would they appear out of nowhere? Would they start shooting at him? We already knew they had guns, which meant James was taking a risk.

When he reached the rover, he threw himself behind the vehicle and hid in the tall, yellow grass.

To my surprise, not a single shot was fired.

He waited a few seconds, then rolled over

onto his knees and tried to open the door at the back—something he'd referred to as a trunk.

Nothing happened.

Was it locked? My heart skipped a beat.

Didn't James need a *key* to operate the rover? He'd grab one every morning before our runs from inside the parking garage.

How could he possibly start the rover without that key?

I didn't vocalize my fear.

James knew what he was doing, I reminded myself.

Surely, he would have thought about the fact that he didn't have the key.

I watched him as he crawled around the side. It was a strange technique, especially since he was carrying the panel. Rather than hold it against his chest the way Dax had done, he laid it flat in the grass and, every few seconds, lifted it and threw it ahead a few more inches.

He worked his way to the front door and reached for the handle.

When he pulled, nothing happened. But I wasn't surprised. Why would the front be any different if the trunk door hadn't opened?

James suddenly lay down, disappearing into the grass.

When he got back up, he held something shiny in his hands.

I couldn't tell what it was from this distance, but I assumed he'd pulled some sort of tool out of his pocket. He then did something that confused me even more—he stuck that shiny metal thing inside the rover's front door.

What was he doing?

His head shook from side to side as he struggled with something.

I turned to look at Dax, who tilted her head to one side with one eye bigger than the other.

"What's he doing—" I started.

"I have no idea," she said.

As I watched him struggle with the front door, I couldn't help but wish he'd move faster. If Dax was right, and the shooters from the other side of the river had anticipated where we were going, then it wouldn't be long before they found us.

I looked away from James, shifting my focus to the other side. "You see anything?"

Dax crossed her arms. "Nothing."

We came out of the forest a little bit. If James needed a distraction, our enemy needed to either see us or hear us. Although I didn't want bullets coming our way, I felt safe at this distance. My feelings may have been irrational, given that I knew nothing about guns or how far bullets could fly.

The next thing I knew, the front door of the rover swung open. Still crouched in the grass,

James reached inside, and the trunk's door opened next.

I smiled at Dax.

Maybe he didn't need the key, after all.

James made his way to the trunk, reached inside, then came back out with a strange, metal-looking rope. It reminded me of the same stuff I'd seen in Fort Denton—what others had referred to as *wire*.

When he returned to the front of the rover, he grabbed the panel, then moved toward the *hood*.

He reached up, wiggled something, and the top of the hood suddenly came undone and went straight up into the air. It was a very odd sight. Had he broken something?

James went to work using the wires he'd collected from the trunk.

Obviously, he knew what he was doing—attaching wires in certain places and connecting them to the solar panel. When he finished, he slid the panel over the hood and started wrapping it up with more wire, securing it in place.

When he finished, he slammed the hood closed.

Even from this distance, I heard the *clunk*.

But that sound was quiet in comparison to what came next.

Suddenly, gunshots went off, and James started flailing his arms around. He hurried to the rover's side, jumped into the driver's seat, and slammed the door shut.

At the same time, Dax ran out of the forest and started shooting wildly.

Bang, bang, bang.

What was she shooting at? I couldn't see anyone.

And I wasn't so sure she could, either.

She fired bullets until the only sound that came out of the gun was a strange clicking noise.

What did *that* mean?

With wide brown eyes, Dax came running back toward me. At the same time, patches of dirt started spitting up toward the sky as bullets came our way.

So bullets can come this far. My initial comfort disappeared immediately.

"Go, go, go!" Dax shouted.

She grabbed me by the arm and we bolted back into the forest together.

"What about James?" I shouted.

It wasn't long before we stopped running. We had only run far enough to get out of their line of sight.

"James knows what he's doing," Dax said, catching her breath. "And I'm sure they don't want to damage their own rover, so they won't shoot at it while he's in there."

How did we even know Jared's men were shooting at us? What if it was someone else?

Someone who didn't care whether or not the rover got damaged?

When the bullets stopped, I looked over at Dax. Maybe she was right. They weren't shooting anymore. Was it because it was, in fact, Jared's soldiers, and they had been instructed not to damage the rover?

"He just needs to start the thing and drive away," Dax said.

Was it really *that* simple? Did the solar panel have an instant effect?

"He doesn't have a key," I said.

Dax's eyes popped out. "What? Why didn't you tell me this? What the hell is he doing, then?"

Dax's fear only made mine worse. Even *she* knew that a key was required, and she hadn't come with us on our trips. Maybe she'd learned a thing or two in Fort Denton.

"What are you saying?" I asked.

With a thin line for lips, she aimed her terrified gaze toward James. "Well, we can't keep standing here. We have to help him."

CHAPTER 20

My fingers ached as I loaded my crossbow.

Dax stared at her gun and sighed. "It's empty."

"Empty?" I asked.

"Out of ammo."

"Ammo?" I asked.

I felt stupid for even questioning her, given that it wasn't the time or place for me to be learning new words. But at the same time, I needed to know what she was talking about, especially in a dangerous situation like this.

"It's ammunition, Silver," she said impatiently. "It just means bullets. I can't use this, and Sadie was the only other one with a weapon."

The sound of Sadie's name caused my stomach to knot. Pushing the thought away, I said, "It's okay. I'll go."

Preparing my crossbow, I crouched the way James had done, trying to blend in with the grass. As I moved closer toward the river, I saw them. About six were on the other side of the river; all were dressed in black, and I couldn't tell who they were or if any of them looked familiar from this distance.

But there they stood with their gazes fixed on James and the rover. One of them pointed at him and then at something on the ground. Then, another man next to him slid off his shirt, revealing large bulging muscles beneath golden brown skin, and removed his boots. What was he doing? Was he—

Without warning, he dove headfirst into the river.

It barely made a splash, and I wondered how long it would take him to get across. With muscles like his, I imagined he'd reach James in no time.

Dax had been right. They didn't want to shoot the rover, but that wouldn't stop them from getting to the other side to kill James. And James was unarmed.

Keeping as low as possible, I hurried toward the rover.

The men carrying guns seemed too preoccupied with James and their swimming friend to even look my way.

I moved awkwardly, my crossbow's metal frame slamming into my thigh repeatedly. It didn't hurt, but it made my movements that much more difficult.

What was this man planning to do, anyway? Although I'd seen him hand his gun over to someone, it didn't mean he was defenseless.

I squinted at the rover's window, trying to see what James was up to. But all I saw was the blue sky's reflection and hundreds of grass blades dancing in the wind.

I couldn't see anything—only reflections.

As I moved closer, a figure appeared on the opposite side of the river. As he climbed up the river's edge, the man grew taller and taller. He was wet from head to toe when he appeared in full view. He ran a hand through his medium-length hair, combing it to one side.

The man was huge.

His size easily made James look like a child.

Smiling, he approached the rover as if meeting up with a friend.

He didn't look afraid at all. If anything, he seemed to be enjoying this.

Planting two hands on his hips, he said, "Get out of the vehicle, and no one gets hurt."

His smirk told me he was the type of person who enjoyed confrontation, and I supposed that was why they'd sent *him* to this side. It was one thing to shoot a gun, but it was quite another to drag someone out of a vehicle and beat them.

As he spoke, his chest muscles bulged, and I couldn't tell if he was doing it on purpose to intimidate James or if they were simply tightening as he spoke.

He moved slowly toward the rover, tilting sideways to glimpse through the front window.

"I see you sitting there, little guy," he said. "I also see that you managed to turn the engine on without a key." He jiggled a little black key between his fingers.

The engine.

Only then did I notice the faint rumbling sound coming from the rover.

If the engine was running, why wasn't James driving away? Had he seen me approach? Was he afraid to leave me behind? I suddenly felt stupid for having come out this way. I should have trusted him.

Without warning, the large man ran to the passenger door and pulled.

The handle loudly clicked, but the door didn't open.

"Unlock the doors," the man ordered.

James didn't react.

Slowly, the man made his way to the driver's side, and I dropped into the grass, flat on my stomach.

The earth underneath me felt cool and hard against my beating chest.

I couldn't see much of the man anymore—only his broad shoulders and the back of his head, and thick neck.

"I'm going to count to three," he said, gently knocking on James's window. "If you surrender, we'll go easy on you. But if you make me use this key"—he waved it in the air as if threatening to cut James with it—"let's just say I'll take my time with you."

Still, James didn't move.

"One," the man said.

I gripped my crossbow with my sweaty palms.

I only had one shot. If I missed, that monster of a man would crush me.

"Two."

But I had to try... I had to do something, even though I was terrified.

I squeezed my eyes shut, feeling dizzy.

"Three."

The man leaned forward, preparing to insert his key into the rover's door.

I immediately raised myself onto my knees, aimed my crossbow at his back, and fired.

The bowstring snapped, and the bolt pierced the man's back, right in the middle. He froze, and I couldn't tell whether he was surprised and barely harmed or about to collapse to his knees.

"Silver!" came James's voice.

A loud metallic sound echoed next to my cheek, and something burned my forehead. Next, I was thrown to the ground forcefully.

My ear rang. I reached for my forehead, a searing pain burning my skull.

What... what had happened? And where

was my crossbow?

Then, I spotted it in the grass next to me. But it wasn't intact anymore, and a huge chunk appeared to be missing from it.

Someone had shot my crossbow. They'd almost killed me.

Then, the noise continued.

Bang.

Bang.

Bang.

Dirt spat up all around me. At the same time, the large man fell to his knees, then collapsed to his side.

"Get in!" James shouted.

Where was his voice coming from? What was he talking about? I squinted as dirt sprinkled into my eyes.

"Silver!"

I followed his voice—it had come from a slit in the black window.

"Get in the back!"

Crawling on my stomach, I moved to the back passenger door of the rover. Before I could even reach for the handle, it opened slightly. I opened the rest of it, and James pulled his arm back to the front of the rover.

"Get in! Get in!"

As I climbed in, the gunshots stopped.

"Close the door!"

I did as I was told.

"Are you hurt?" he asked.

I couldn't move or speak. What had just happened? Everything spun around me, and I blinked hard to regain my grip on reality.

"Silver!"

"I-I'm okay," I said, tapping my body.

There was no blood. I was okay, right? Or had I been shot?

I wasn't sure. Adrenaline coursed through me, and it felt as though I'd disconnected from my body for a moment.

"But they shot my crossbow," I finally said.

"Forget your crossbow!" he shouted.

He gripped and regripped the steering wheel—a high-pitched, leathery sound.

Slowly, I sat upright, wanting to catch a glimpse of our attackers.

Then, through the front window, I saw *him*. Jared.

He stood taller than everyone else, his shoulders hunched forward and bouncing as he breathed hard. Next to his sides, his fingers curled as if he were holding on to invisible rocks.

He looked so angry.

When his men raised their guns at us, he waved a hand, ordering them not to shoot.

"Why aren't they shooting?" I asked. "Dax said something about not wanting to damage the rover."

"Exactly," James said. "We don't have the resources to build more of these. If they destroy it, they're only hurting themselves. And now that the solar panel is attached, it's an extra risk for them. They can't risk damaging the panel *or* the rover."

"And why are we still here?" I said, impatient.

Suddenly, Jared raised a hand and clicked his fingers, and three more of his men slipped out of their shirts and boots.

"Um, James... Why aren't we moving?"

"We can't yet," he said. "Look."

He pointed at the bright lights in front of the steering wheel.

"Remember how I told you about the energy reservoir? It's a tiny bump over empty. The panel is working, but it's not an instant fix. It still takes time to charge."

I swallowed hard, my throat sticking to itself.

"But they're coming," I said.

James's sunglasses tipped upward as he watched me through the rearview mirror. "Did you grab the key?"

I shook my head. "What? No. I didn't even think—"

Without warning, James swung his door open but didn't step out. He waited, almost as if testing Jared. And it was good that he'd done that because Jared didn't hesitate to point a gun our way.

"What are you doing?" I asked. "You can't go

out there."

"I'm not," James said. "The guy fell right here." He grumbled his last words as he stretched down into the grass, reaching for the key.

When he returned, he flashed the key at me in his mirror and smirked. "This'll make getting around much easier. Don't get me wrong, hotwiring worked, but it's not a long-term solution."

"Hotwiring?" I asked.

He shook his head as if to say, *Don't worry about it. Doesn't matter.*

I stared wide-eyed at the energy reservoir, my breathing shallow. A little green bar flickered. One second, it was there, and the next, it was gone.

"Why is it doing that?" I asked.

"It's charging," he said. "One more bar, and we should be good to drive for about forty miles. Enough to get us away from them." He jerked his chin out at Jared.

Suddenly, three wet heads appeared in the distance. They bounced gently as the men walked toward us, and within seconds, their bare chests came into view.

"Um, James..."

"Just a bit more..." James muttered under his breath.

I blinked hard.

A bit more?

We didn't have the time for a bit *more*.

And judging from Jared's angry posture, I was beginning to think he'd told his men to break a window if necessary. Without my crossbow, we had nothing.

As the men drew in closer, James hunched over his wheel as if trying to increase the charging speed with his mind.

But it wasn't working.

The little green light kept flickering at the same speed.

"We can't just sit here!" I shouted.

I glanced through the front window to spot the men moving toward us with clenched fists.

The one in the middle reached for a handle on his belt and pulled out a large, shiny knife.

"James!" I shouted.

The green bar suddenly stopped flickering.

"Got it!" he shouted.

He shifted the gear stick and slammed on the Go pedal.

For a moment, it felt like we were driving in one spot.

Maybe we were. James had mentioned something about wheels spinning when a lot of sudden power was involved. Behind us, blades of grass flew upward, and the men broadened their shoulders in front of us as they shouted.

I couldn't tell if they were preparing to jump out of the way, back into the river, or throw themselves at the rover.

But it didn't matter.

James spun the steering wheel so fast that within seconds, the men were now on the rover's side, then at the back, and then small figures in the distance. They chased after us, but they were no match for the rover's speed.

CHAPTER 21

I pointed through the rover's front window. "Right there!"

James had already seen her. He turned the steering wheel until we were facing Dax and sped up. Behind us, the men were still running. What were they hoping to achieve?

Bang!

Wood chunks flew off a tree next to Dax's head, and her eyes went huge.

Then, James did something a horse certainly couldn't do. He came at Dax quickly and spun his steering wheel in the opposite direction at the very last second. The rover slid sideways until the back landed right in front of Dax, shielding her from our enemies.

Without being told what to do, she opened the back door and jumped in headfirst.

"Holy!" she shouted, her voice bouncing off the rover's interior walls. "Did you guys see that? He missed me by an inch!" She brushed her short brown hair back and stared up at the ceiling. "I even felt my hair move when the bullet flew by."

It was almost like it had excited her.

Dax blew out a breath. "That was way too close—"

James slammed his foot on the pedal, and she flew against the back seat.

She didn't seem bothered by it. If anything, it only excited her more. With a grin, she sat upright and started petting the leather interior. She then slid a finger along the door's interior, drew a line up to the window, and stared through it.

"It's so dark...."

"It's tint," James said.

"You might want to put that on," I cut in, wiggling a finger at Dax's seatbelt.

It took her a few minutes to figure out how it worked, but when she did, a soft clicking sound confirmed that she was buckled in.

"You guys like suspense, don't you?" she said.

I didn't understand what she meant by this, but James looked at her in his little mirror.

"That wasn't for suspense," he said. "The charge wasn't high enough for us to drive away."

Dax scratched her head. "What charge? From the solar panel?"

He nodded.

Before he could say anything, she leaned

forward and started pointing at something in front of James.

"What's that?"

"The fuel gauge," he said.

"And is that... is that a gear shifter?" she asked.

James smirked and nodded again.

"What about that?" Dax continued.

They went on like this for several minutes, seeming to enjoy the rover-related conversation.

We drove until we reached Logan's house—a once blue, isolated home sitting neatly on a large lot. But now, it was burned almost entirely, with only a few metal beams still standing upright. Everything else had turned to ash or had formed piles of burned wood.

I felt awful for Logan, his wife, and their three children.

They'd seemed like kind people who hadn't deserved to get caught up in Jared's hatred for me. At least now, they were safe in Lockridge with Ari and her people.

James slowed the engine and started driving toward Logan's old barn and stable at the back of the property.

"Why are we stopping here?" I asked.

He sighed. "We're already running out of power. We need to let the rover charge. I thought we could hide behind the barn."

No one argued, so James drove slowly

across Logan's property, hitting a few bumps along the way. He evaded large items such as a broken wooden chair and what appeared to be a couch cushion. I wasn't sure how things had ended up so far across the property, but I imagined the wind was to blame.

Suddenly, we went over something hard, and Dax grunted. "What was that?" She twirled in her seat to get a view through the rear window.

"I don't know," James said. "But the rover can handle it."

It happened a few more times and wasn't a nice feeling. Every time, I wondered if we'd hit something big enough to damage the vehicle. With all the tall grass, it was impossible to see specific items.

"Here we go," James said, pulling around a huge barn full of hay.

James was the first to get out and inhale a lungful of air.

I did the same, appreciating the smell of farmland. It reminded me of home—mostly of Grandma—and Ortus, my new home.

As Dax stepped out of the rover, I said, "How long until it's ready to drive again? We need to go look for Sadie."

Dax nodded, agreeing with me. "If we wait until sunset, things will only worsen for her. It'll get cold, and if she is injured, it won't be easy for her to find shelter or heat."

James walked around the rover, past the barn, and disappeared into a stable—a tall gray structure that was easily twice the size of the one we had in Ortus. Overhead, birds flew about, chirping as their little wings worked hard to get from one end of the barn to the other. On the floor was a bunch of dirt mixed with hay and woodchips.

Where had James gone, anyway? Was he ignoring us? Did he think going after Sadie was a bad idea?

"James," I called out.

He swung around fast with a finger pointing upward—his way of saying, *Hold on a second. Be quiet.*

Then, I heard it—the sound of a horse neighing.

Next came the sound of hooves smacking against compacted dirt.

James smirked back at us. "Rover might be out of commission for the next two hours, but nothing's stopping us from going old-school."

"Old-school?" Dax said, scrunching her nose. "What does that even mean—"

"You know... an old method," James said.

Dax didn't seem convinced, and neither was I. She raised a brow at me, then stared at James. "How are horses old-school?" she asked. "They've been around for centuries, and they're still our primary method of transportation."

James shrugged. "Well, not in Fort Denton."

"So that makes you more advanced than us?" Dax said. "And we're what? Stupid? Simple people?"

I sensed the tension rising, so I stepped in. "Words are just words. I don't think he meant it like that, Dax."

James's smile faded as if Dax had taken all the fun out of everything.

"I wasn't trying to offend anyone," he said. "I just mean we have a highly advanced rover that we can't even use right now. So, we should stick to a more basic means of transportation until the rover is working again."

Dax didn't say anything.

She didn't have to.

I understood exactly why she'd reacted defensively. The people of Lutum had always been viewed as a lower class—as a group of unintelligent simpletons who knew nothing about anything, including how to speak. Only the select few who took the time to read and ask questions ever advanced.

Maybe Dax felt like she'd missed a lot of learning in life. I understood. There was still so much I didn't know, and I hated feeling stupid whenever I had to ask someone to clarify. But it was better to feel stupid for a moment than to live without knowing half of what the rest of the world knew.

I'd choose temporary discomfort over

being permanently uneducated.

Trying to clear the tense air, I brushed past Dax and moved ahead of James toward the stable stalls. Most were empty, and it wasn't until we reached the last one that we found the source of the neighing.

Inside the stall was a beautiful brown horse with a white triangle on her forehead. She wasn't large, but she wasn't small, either. All around her was hay and a lot of manure.

Poor thing. Why hadn't anyone come back for her? Her coat, dusty and uncombed, made her look sickly.

Quietly, I unlatched the gate and slowly opened it. The creaking sound was enough for her to take a few big steps back. She watched me with her huge brown eyes, and I couldn't help but stare into them.

"It's okay," I whispered. "You're okay."

I reached for her snout to pet her, but she pulled away fast and neighed furiously at me.

In the back of my mind, I hoped nothing had happened to Logan or his family. Or Lockridge, for that matter. Why hadn't they come back to save their horse?

Craning my neck, I searched the side of the stall, then the top, until I found a flat piece of wood with the name Beauty burned into it.

"Beauty," I said softly.

Her soft eyes focused on me.

"We're here to get you out," I said.

Behind me, James fidgeted with his fingers and flinched every time Beauty made any sort of noise.

"Can you wait outside?" Dax told him.

An eyebrow popped over his sunglasses. "Why?"

"Because horses can sense everything," she said. "Including your fear. I think you're making this worse."

James waved a hand as if to say, *Yeah, yeah,* and left the stable.

Sadie had been the one to teach us about horse sensitivity. It had taken me some time to let go of my fear, but once I did, everything changed.

"You're right," I said. "Let's act like she's ours."

I pushed aside my fear and stepped into the stall with a smile.

"Hey there, Beauty," I said, petting her snout.

She stared at me.

She still wasn't sure, but it was better than earlier.

"How do you know she's ridable?" Dax asked.

I shrugged. "I don't, but we have to find out." I searched behind Dax's head, where all sorts of equipment hung on a weathered, gray wall.

"There," I said, pointing at an oval-shaped

brush.

She handed it to me, and I started grooming Beauty.

She seemed to enjoy it until I reached her back, where countless insect bites had formed little red bumps. Big black flies circled her, threatening to land and take another chunk of her skin. Without a word, I shooed them away. But they were hungry and kept coming back.

"Let's get her out of here," I said.

Dax reached for a red halter hanging from a whole set of them on the wall. Underneath these were two saddles—one large and black, the other a bit smaller and made of brown leather. She reached for the smaller one, then helped me put the gear on Beauty.

It wasn't easy.

Beauty pulled her head away every few seconds, trying to avoid the leather straps.

After the third attempt, Dax sighed. "Maybe that's why they didn't come back for her."

She sounded defeated like we should give up and leave her behind.

"Doesn't matter," I said. "We have to try. And if we can't ride her, she's better off running wild than she is rotting away in this stall."

Dax didn't argue.

She knew I was right.

When Beauty was all set up with her riding gear, I opened the thick wooden stall door and led her out. It took me a few nudges to get her moving, but she followed me, even though she didn't seem to want to.

She walked across the dirt floor, her hooves occasionally landing on cement and causing a loud clicking sound to resonate throughout the stable.

Overhead, a few birds chirped and flew from one end of the stable to the other.

Beauty's head snapped sideways at the sound. I pulled her lead to give her head a good tug, and she recentered.

Although I felt somewhat confident with horses, I knew Sadie would have better managed this horse. But that didn't matter right now because Sadie wasn't here. It was on me to make this work if I wanted to get my friend back.

When we stepped out of the stable, Beauty's big brown eyes closed halfway as she took in the afternoon sun. Dozens of flies followed her out, and her skin twitched every time they landed on her. She'd turn her head back quickly to bite at them.

"Hold still," I breathed, then tugged on the strap that held her saddle in place—a *cinch*, Sadie had called it—to ensure the saddle would stay on tightly.

I didn't bother asking Dax if she wanted to be the one to ride because I knew that I wouldn't stop searching until I found Sadie.

It had to be me.

Gripping the saddle, I placed my foot into the stirrup.

I was thankful for Beauty's size—getting up wasn't as hard as mounting certain Ortus horses.

I pulled myself up and landed with a thump in the saddle. At once, Beauty neighed and stomped her hooves.

I froze, waiting.

I'd be okay if she didn't take off running.

"You sure this is a good idea?" Dax asked.

James stood at a safe distance, watching me behind his shades. He kept quiet, almost as if afraid that the wrong word might set the horse off.

"I have to try," I said. "If I'm not back in a few hours, head to Lockridge without me."

"A few hours?" Dax blurted. "You need to be more specific than that."

I searched the stable, the barn in the distance, and the ground. Next to the stable's entrance was an oversized nail planted into the dirt. It looked like something Logan might have used to tie up his dog. It stood several inches high, resulting in a thin shadow stretching toward Dax's feet.

I pointed at it.

"By the time that shadow hits the stable's entrance," I said. "If I'm not back by then, go to Lockridge for Westin. Tell him what happened. He has the right to know about his father."

Dax looked at the nail and nodded.

I gave Beauty's reins a slight tug and squeezed her sides with my legs.

She didn't budge.

Dax blinked, staring at the horse with her hands on her hips. "Maybe she was never taught."

I stared back at her. What if she was right? What if this horse hadn't been properly broken?

I squeezed harder this time and made a clicking sound with my mouth—a sound Sadie had taught me.

Nothing.

The horse let out a big lungful of air like it was annoyed with me.

"Come on, Beauty," I said. "We have to—"

Out of nowhere, she took off at full speed.

CHAPTER 22

I squinted as we traveled fast through the open field.

My hair flew behind me, swimming through the air. I leaned forward a bit, not because I wanted to help the horse go faster—something about balance and wind reduction—but because it was the only position that made me feel safe. I was afraid that if I sat up upright, I'd fall off.

"Slow down!" I shouted.

She wasn't stopping.

To make matters worse, she wasn't even moving toward the river.

"Beauty!"

I pulled hard on the reins.

It aggravated her, but she didn't stop running.

I tugged again, bouncing wildly as I tried to gain control of her.

Nothing.

So instead, I tugged only on one side,

confusing her and causing her to turn sharply. To my surprise, it slowed her down a bit, so I continued directing her from one side to the other until all we did was spin in circles in the middle of nowhere.

At least she was listening.

"Easy," I said, petting her neck.

Her ears moved from front to back, again and again.

She was afraid. She kept hearing things and didn't know whether they were a threat.

Wanting to keep her busy, I started moving straight again. Every time she looked like she was about to take off, I gave a good tug and refocused her attention on making a turn.

It worked well.

So well that I eventually made it to the river.

I was far away from the broken bridge and couldn't imagine Jared and his men coming out this far. Then again, I couldn't be sure. I glanced across the river through the trees and tall grass every few moments. I wanted to call out for Sadie, but I was too afraid.

What if they were waiting across the river? And now that I knew how far bullets could travel, I didn't exactly want to attract any attention from my enemies.

"Sadie," I whispered, walking my horse along a row of cat tails. Or were they cattails? Sadie had spelled it out for me, but I recalled that it sounded like a cat's tail.

The long, fuzzy, brown plants looked nothing like a cat's tail. At least, not like the cat I'd seen in Fort Denton's library. That tail had been swirly, long, and fluffy.

I wished Grandma were here to see this.

In a way, I wished Mother were here, too.

If only she could see me riding this horse, searching for my friend, and trying to help the people of Ortus.

Would she be proud of me? Or, would she call me useless and retreat into herself as she so often did?

It doesn't matter. Grandma was always proud of me, and that's all that matters.

I inhaled a deep breath, pushing down my feelings of grief and sadness. I missed Grandma so much, but most days, I didn't allow myself to truly feel it. It was easier to focus on everyone else—the Elites, the people of Ortus, Sadie, my friends.

The last thing I wanted was to turn out like Mother—a bitter woman who treated others poorly due to her own misery.

"Sadie," I tried again, my sharp voice slipping through the countless cattails.

A strong breeze swept by, tilting the cattails in one direction.

At the same time, Beauty's ears rotated forward, and she perked up.

"Easy," I said, petting the side of her neck.

If something spooked her, there was no telling how long it would take to regain control.

Before she could focus on whatever she had heard, I pulled sideways and changed my course.

How far downriver could Sadie have gone? Had she swum along the edge, or had the current taken her?

I felt queasy at the thought. I remembered how strong the water had been and how I'd been unable to swim out of it.

But Sadie knows how to swim. I don't.

I fought with my mind for hours as I trotted up and down the river, calling out to Sadie.

Overhead, the sun had reached the center of the sky and was now beginning its descent.

Sadie's strong, I told myself. She'll be okay.

I fought back tears and the thought of her dead body floating in the river.

Grandma had always taught me that our minds were the cause of most of our worries. She'd explained that humans could create all sorts of false scenarios in their heads, panic about them, and only later realize that their panic had been unnecessary.

I didn't want to panic.

I wanted to be strong, like Grandma.

But it was hard.

I breathed in deep and led Beauty away from the river. If I didn't make it back to Logan's stables, Dax and James would leave without me. And as much as I wanted to find Sadie, I also didn't want to be alone in the middle of nowhere with Jared still possibly hunting us.

The only safe place to be was in Lockridge, with Ari and her people.

The village was hidden from view, and they had shelter, food, water, and protection.

Maybe tomorrow... I could try again.

I led Beauty back toward the stables, wanting nothing more than to cry. I missed Sadie, and I needed to know she was okay. Where was she, and why hadn't I been able to find her?

When I reached the stables, Dax threw her arms in the air and sighed. "Did you have to wait until the very last minute?"

I wasn't sure what she was talking about.

She pointed at the large nail in the ground; its shadow was now grazing the stable's entryway.

"You told us if you weren't back by—"

I waved a hand and climbed off of Beauty. "I know, I'm sorry. I just wanted to keep looking."

Dax reached for Beauty's lead, but Beauty pulled away and let out a frustrated sound.

"Okay," Dax said, raising two flat palms next to her face. "I guess she doesn't want anyone handling her but you."

I smiled weakly at Beauty and patted her neck again.

James suddenly flung the rover's door open and stepped out. When he closed it, Beauty jumped back several feet, and it took me several minutes to calm her down.

"Someone's jumpy," he said, straightening the sunglasses on his face. He then swept a hand through his golden hair and stared at us like he was waiting for something.

When neither of us said anything, he added, "Well?"

"Well, what?" I said.

"We have enough energy to get to Lockridge," he said. "You both ready?"

I looked at Dax, who nodded, then at the rover, and then up at Beauty.

"She won't fit," James said, and it didn't sound like he was joking, either.

I clenched my teeth. Did he really expect me to leave her behind? How would she survive on her own? Suddenly, I remembered Maz's horses—the ones we'd left tied in the forest on the other side of the river. I hoped that Jared hadn't found them and taken them as his own.

"We shouldn't have all crossed," I said.

Dax raised an eyebrow as if I'd told her the sky was falling.

"The river," I corrected. "You and Sadie should have stayed on the other side and returned to Ortus."

Dax scoffed through her round nose. "Well, that doesn't make any sense. Jared and his men were right behind us. They'd have killed us right there."

I shifted my focus onto Beauty's hooves.

Dax was right.

It was a stupid thought. But all I wanted was to go back in time and stop Sadie from falling into the river. And maybe if that hadn't happened, she could have returned to Ortus with Maz's horses. I didn't like the idea of horses being tied to trees alone. What if wolves found them?

"Well, then we need to hurry," I said. "We can't leave our horses tied up for days in the forest."

Dax planted a firm and heavy hand on my shoulder. At first, she didn't say anything, and it was almost like she was trying to calm me with her touch. "I know, Silver. And we will, okay?"

Was it that obvious I was panicking? There was too much for us to do, and I was afraid we wouldn't be able to do it all.

Not only did we have to get back to our horses, but we had to find Sadie, reunite with Westin in Lockridge and tell him about his father, then find a way back over to Ortus and figure out how to get the rover across. To make matters worse, I couldn't return to Ortus, which meant I'd have to figure out where I would live and how I would survive.

"Hey," James said, throwing his chin out at

me. "One step at a time. Right now, we need to get to Lockridge."

"We also have to find Sadie," I said.

He nodded like he agreed with me, which was reassuring. "Yeah, we do. But we can't do that if we're exhausted, and it's dark out. Our best bet is to ask Ari for a few people to help us search."

James was right. If Sadie was alive, she'd fight for as long as possible to stay that way.

"Okay," I breathed.

James smirked again, his freckled cheeks pushing his sunglasses upward. "Race you there?"

It had come out sounding like a question more than anything.

What was he talking about?

He pointed at Beauty. "Well, we all know you don't have the heart to leave her behind. So, Dax can ride with me, and you can follow."

Beauty let out air through her nostrils like she was satisfied with this plan.

"All right," I said.

Planting my foot in the old stirrup, I pulled myself back onto Beauty's back.

I wanted to joke about how Beauty would probably win the race, but I couldn't find it in me to smile. All I wanted was to find Sadie.

So instead, I fought against the countless awful thoughts in my brain as I followed the rover toward Lockridge.

CHAPTER 23

Pebbles flew out from underneath the rover's wheel as James slowed near Lockridge's wooden sign. It looked the same as it had last time—worn, covered in vines, and pointing in the wrong direction.

Logan had warned us about the sign the first time he gave us directions from his burning house. He'd explained that the sign pointed in the wrong direction on purpose.

It was smart.

Those who knew nothing about Lockridge would make a left turn away from the forest and leave Lockridge and its people alone.

The rover slowly turned to the right, preparing to drive onto Lockridge's forest path, but then abruptly stopped.

What was James doing?

I led Beauty to his window and waited for him to lower it.

When he did, he stuck his head out, the dark lenses of his shades reflecting a distorted version of me atop Beauty.

"What's going on?" I asked.

"Dax wants to make a stop," he said.

A stop? What was that supposed to mean? We were supposed to be stopping in *Lockridge*. Nowhere else.

Dax leaned over, her short messy hair nearly tickling James's chin. She stuck out a long arm, jabbing James in the chest with her elbow, and pointed out his window.

"Look, over there!" she said.

I followed her aim.

In the distance, gray smoke spread from the ground and up into the sky. Like the tornado I'd seen before entering Fort Denton, the smoke was thin at the base and broader at the top.

"What is that?" I asked.

"Looks like smoke," James said. "But from what?"

"Haven't you traveled that way?" I asked.

James once told me he'd traveled most of the land around Fort Denton.

"We never went beyond the river," he reminded me.

Of course, I already knew this, and felt stupid for having asked.

The smoke rose from behind a hill, so we couldn't see what was causing it.

"We should go see," Dax said, still leaning across the centerpiece.

James scrunched his nose at her as if she'd suggested we abandon the rover and light it on fire. "And why would we do that?"

She frowned at him like *he* was the one being stupid.

"Why wouldn't we?" she said. "Someone might need help."

"Or someone might attack us," James pointed out.

"I doubt it," she said.

James scoffed. "How would you know? Maybe someone is watching us, and they're trying to lure us—"

"You haven't been out this way," Dax cut him off. "You said so yourself. So don't sit here and assume the worst. We can be careful about it. Aren't you curious? What if it's Sadie trying to send us a signal?"

My heart skipped a beat. Dax was right. What if this *was* Sadie?

James sighed and gripped the steering wheel repeatedly, his knuckles turning white. Then, he shifted his gaze to me—or at least it looked like it. It was always hard to tell behind those shades of his.

"We can go carefully," I said.

"Fine," James said through clenched teeth.

He spun his steering wheel in the opposite direction and slowly shifted his course. I followed closely, galloping behind the rover as we neared the grassy hill with smoke expanding behind it.

James slowly pulled the rover up to the hill's edge and stopped.

"We can get out here," he said.

Before opening his door, he paused. "Do we even have any weapons?"

Both Dax and I shook our heads at the same time. My crossbow had been shot, and Dax had used up all the bullets in James's gun.

"Then let's be careful," he said.

James and Dax exited the rover quietly, and I climbed off Beauty. She seemed content being tied up to the rover's mirror, and I only hoped she wouldn't try to take off because there was a good chance she'd rip the mirror right off.

Without a sound, we made our way up the hill. I kept my knees bent as if this would somehow quiet my footsteps or keep me hidden.

The smell of burning entered my nostrils.

But it wasn't the burning scent I was used to, like the smell of wood or charcoal. This smell was strong and didn't smell right.

James sniffed the air and frowned. "Smells like—"

"Mechanical," Dax cut in.

James nodded at her.

We hurried up the rest of the hill, then carefully peered over.

"Damn son of a—" came a loud, obnoxious

voice.

The sound of impact followed, like something had been kicked.

I lay on my stomach and crawled up to the top of the hill.

Below was a long yellow vehicle—the bus we'd seen in Lockridge. And next to it was the same round-bellied man who had taken food from Ari and threatened to destroy their village if she didn't offer something better next time.

"Krampus," I whispered through clenched teeth.

He moved around, looking infuriated with his balled fists and small, drawn shoulders. His belly hung out far but didn't jiggle when he walked. It looked hard, like stone. He paced along the bus, fixing his glasses on his face and readjusting his bright blue jacket so aggressively it looked like he was trying to rip it to pieces.

I shifted my focus to the front of the bus, where the smoke came from. It swept out of the big crack at the front of the vehicle—a large gap that made it look broken. Inside were dark bits of metal and other pieces, and although I wasn't sure what they were, I imagined they were necessary for the bus to keep operating.

Krampus stormed to the front, climbed on what looked like a block of wood to get a bit higher, and stuck his head inside the big, dark split, where the smoke was coming out.

"Something's wrong with his bus," James whispered. "Looks like he's trying to fix it."

Krampus jumped off his block of wood and started coughing nonstop. He slapped the air, trying to clear the smoke out of his face, then went on to punch the air several times.

"You piece of junk!" he shouted. He kicked the bus's tire, squealed, grabbed his injured foot, and hopped on one leg.

But what surprised me the most wasn't the damaged bus or Krampus's anger—it was the dozens of heads behind the bus's dirty windows.

His *soldiers*, as Krampus had referred to them.

Why wasn't anyone moving? Why weren't they trying to help him?

Krampus let out another frustrated growl and stormed inside the bus. He returned with what looked like a toolbox and went back to the smoky front. Within minutes, he gave up again. This time, he threw a metallic tool into the grass, grabbed his short curly brown hair, and let out a roar so loud that I instinctively lowered my head farther into the grass.

"Junk! Junk! Junk!" he went off. The bus shook from side to side when he climbed back on. Then, figures started moving.

"Garbage!" his voice continued. "Useless... useless trash!"

Suddenly, something—or someone—came

flying out of the back of the bus. Rather than follow the thrown figure, Krampus stormed back out through the side door and marched his way over to whoever he'd tossed outside.

I expected this person to get up and defend themselves, but they didn't move.

Krampus came at them, kicking, his short legs barely swinging back for each kick.

Still, his victim lay motionless in the grass.

Krampus then bent down and came back up with what looked like a forest green helmet—something you'd see in military history books. He threw the helmet as far as he could, shouting something.

"He is one angry little man," Dax mumbled. "Should we help the other guy—"

"No," I said coldly. "Just wait."

Something about this didn't feel right.

It wasn't until Krampus picked up the limp body that I knew what was going on. The figure was tall, lean, and highly flexible. Krampus then went on to grab the body by the ankles. As if it weighed nothing, he flapped it up and down, repeatedly slamming its head into the ground.

Fluff came flying out of the figure; some floated in the air, while most of it landed in the grass.

"Is that—" James started.

"Like a giant doll?" I said.

He turned his head to look at me. "I was going to say a dummy, but yeah... same thing."

"Because they're dumb?" I said.

James parted his lips like he was preparing to educate me on something, then closed his mouth. A few seconds later, he sighed. "I actually don't know. We found some in an old store a few years back, and it scared me half to death." He threw his chin out toward Krampus. "That dummy doesn't look as fancy or real-looking as the ones I saw, though."

"So they're fake people," I said.

James nodded. "Basically, yes."

"So they're all fake," I said.

"What?" James asked.

"His soldiers," I said, now smiling. "I knew something was off. He doesn't have protection. He doesn't have anything. He's just a liar."

James looked at me. "I—"

"Dax, do you still have the gun?" I said.

Dax, who lay with her chin in her palms as if she was watching something amusing, snapped back to reality. "Oh, yeah, but it's useless. We don't have any ammo left."

"I don't care," I said. "Give it to me."

"But—"

I gave her a look that told her I wasn't in the mood to argue.

She hesitated, then reached next to her and handed me the gun.

It was cold to the touch. Although I'd been afraid of it earlier, I wasn't now, maybe because there weren't any bullets in it, or maybe because my anger toward Krampus was stronger than my fear of guns.

"What are you going to do?" Dax said. "He could be armed."

I scoffed. "If he has to pretend to have an army in his bus so he can steal from people, he isn't armed."

I jumped upright, slapped a bit of grass off my knees, and started marching toward Krampus.

"Wait!" Dax said. "What aren't you understanding? You can't *use* the gun. It won't shoot."

I smirked back at her. "I don't plan on shooting him. I only want to give him his own taste—"

I paused, feeling like I'd somehow messed up the saying I'd heard in Fort Denton.

"A taste of his own medicine," James said, smiling.

I pointed the gun at James. "Yeah, that."

"Whoa!" he said, throwing his hands up next to his face. "Rule number one about holding a gun—never point it at anyone, even if it's empty or unloaded."

I immediately dropped the gun to my side. "I was going to point it at Krampus."

"Yeah, that's okay," James said. "Because you're threatening him. I mean, never point it at anyone unless you aren't afraid to shoot."

Even Dax was smiling now, and I couldn't

help but smile back.

"My point is that Krampus doesn't know I have an empty gun. He threatened Ari and her people, and this whole time, it was a—"

"Bluff," James helped me.

"It was a bluff," I repeated. "So now, I'll bluff him."

James rubbed his forehead and tightened his lips to hide his smile. It was like he didn't want to embarrass me for my poor choice of words.

I wanted to ask him what I'd said wrong, but I didn't want to waste any more time.

So instead, I tightened my grip around the gun and started marching straight down the hill toward the angry little man.

CHAPTER 24

Krampus's eyes went huge, almost as if he thought I was a wolf coming to eat him. He froze, his chubby hands hanging on either side of his rounded belly. He held a bunch of white fluff in one fist—material he'd ripped out of the doll, or dummy, as James had referred to it—and a tuft of grass in the other.

"Whoa," he said, taking a step back.

He dropped the white fluff in the grass, pulled his shoulders back, and narrowed his eyes into little slits full of judgment. For a moment, I thought he might start yelling at me for spooking him. It was almost like he wanted to accuse me of being rude for interrupting what he was doing.

With nostrils flared, he raised a tight fist at me and shook it.

But the anger on his face instantly vanished when he saw my gun.

His confidence melted, and he took several steps back.

"Oh, um—" he stammered.

He reached for the bus's open back door with his short arm.

What was he trying to do? Hide behind it? Or maybe he was getting ready to jump back inside the bus and lock the doors.

He tripped on his own shoes, his curly hair dancing atop his head. Less than gracefully, he caught himself on the door and nearly smashed his face into it. The hinges made a loud creaking sound, and slowly, he stepped behind it.

"Don't," I said, pointing the empty gun at him.

It felt weird, given that I'd never held a gun before. And I certainly had never threatened anyone with a gun. It was so small and compact. How could such a tiny thing take someone's life? I stopped staring at the weapon and focused my attention on Krampus.

"You lied," I said.

He laughed nervously—a high-pitched sound—and forced a wide smile that looked like it didn't belong on his face, or any human's face.

"Wh-what? What are you talking about?"

I pointed the gun at the ripped dummy and then back up at him. "You don't have an army. You don't have anything. And you're stealing from Ari and a lot of innocent people."

Then, out of nowhere, he fell to his knees

and started crying like a child. He pulled at his curly locks, his round face darkening several shades of red as he sobbed. His cheeks glistened with tears, and a snot bubble ballooned out of his left nostril.

"Please, don't kill me! Don't kill me!" he shrieked. "It's... It's not my fault! I have to. You don't understand."

"You *have* to?" I asked. "Why do you have to threaten an entire village for food?"

Without looking at me, he waved his arms wildly, then slapped his thighs. "You don't understand. It's not me. It's *him*. He'll kill me if I don't do it. It's not my fault!"

I parted my lips to ask him who he was talking about, but he let out an ear-splitting shriek and covered his face with his swollen little hands. "Don't shoot!"

I lowered my gun. "Would you calm down?"

He peered at me through a crack in his fingers.

When he noticed I wasn't aiming the gun at him anymore, he cleared his throat, stood again, and slapped grass from his knees.

"I, um, I believe there's been a misunderstanding." He stuck his chin in the air, regaining his confidence.

I got the feeling that if I were to lift James's gun again, he'd drop to his knees and start squealing.

"I was only following orders," he said, his

nose still up in the air.

Did he think that excused his behavior? That what he'd done was okay because someone else had told him to?

"You lied to a bunch of people," I said, getting angry.

I preferred him on his knees, looking sorry for what he'd done.

He let out a forced laugh and patted his belly. "Yes, yes, I know. I—" Pausing, he glanced at my gun. "It was... wrong. I should have never done that."

I got the feeling he wasn't being sincere at all. As if any second, he'd laugh out loud and say that it was all Ari's fault for being stupid enough to believe his lies.

I didn't like this man very much.

He seemed like a bad person who didn't care for anyone but himself.

"Truce?" he said, probably sensing how angry I was with him.

He offered me his hand and smiled broadly. Before I could tell him to keep his germs to himself, footsteps echoed behind me.

James approached with a scowl, and Dax looked as menacing.

"Everything okay?" James said.

His voice was more formal than usual, and he stood with his chest puffed out. The look didn't suit him—James was very kind and sweet on the inside—but I appreciated that he was trying to look intimidating for me. He wanted Krampus to think he was a dangerous guy and that he wasn't afraid to use his muscles if needed.

Not that he'd need them. The gun in my hand seemed to be the only threat any of us needed against Krampus.

"Yeah," Dax added, also coming across as tough. "This guy giving you any trouble?"

Krampus took a step back like a coward, his grin widening so much it was a wonder his gums didn't dry out completely. "Oh, h-hello there."

He positioned himself with his back against the bus and his little hands flat against the yellow metal on either side of him.

When neither James nor Dax responded, Krampus added, "We're just sorting out a few differences."

Dax crossed her muscular arms and watched him carefully. She looked angrier than she had when she'd been watching Krampus from the top of the hill. James must have told her the whole story about Krampus and his treacheries.

"The only differences you need to sort out are with Ari," I said.

Krampus scrunched his nose. "Who's Ari—" I must have frowned hard at him because he let out a choppy, high-pitched giggle and said, "Oh, yes, of course. Of course. Ari. Yes, the um... the lady in charge..." He watched me as if trying to gauge how close he was to the truth.

He didn't remember Ari's name, did he?

I considered yelling at him for being so thoughtless, but there was no point. What mattered now was finding out who was behind all of this. Krampus had mentioned that someone else was threatening him. So, who was it?

"Who sends you to collect food from Lockridge?" I asked.

"Lockridge..." he mumbled.

"The village on the edge of the water!" I shouted.

I tightened my grip around my gun, and his eyes followed my whitening knuckles.

"Oh!" he shrieked, his eyes popping open wide. "I, um, I'm just a little nervous." He wiggled his finger at my gun. "You know, around guns. I-I'm sorry for my bad memory."

I didn't believe him. I now got the feeling that he stole from several places and couldn't keep track of any names.

Did that mean there were other villages around here? Other people? If so, were they friendly?

I shook these thoughts away and focused on Krampus.

"Who sends you?" I asked again.

His big blue eyes darted from side to side. It was like he was afraid to give me any information at all. Either that or like someone was listening to our conversation. I looked around us, then threw my arms out on either side of me, my gun following. "What are you so worried about? There's no one out here."

"Maybe not..." he said. "But if I get this person in trouble, he'll have my head."

"Have your head?" I repeated. What did that even mean?

He slid a thumb across his throat with bulging eyes and tongue hanging out.

"He'll kill you," I said.

Krampus raised a brow at me, probably trying to figure out where I came from.

I wasn't in the mood to have to explain myself, so I made my eyes go big, and he shrieked again.

"Yes! Yes! That's what I meant. I assumed everyone knew that saying, but I suppose I don't know where you people are from."

Neither Dax nor James said anything behind me. They knew I was leading this conversation and would only step in if asked.

I pointed my gun at Krampus again, and instantly, he fell to his knees and started crying out like a baby bird begging to be fed. "No, please! Please!"

"Well, if you don't answer me, you're dead anyway," I said.

I didn't recognize myself as the words came out of my mouth. I imagined what I looked like to him, frowning and holding a gun. Not long ago, I'd been an innocent child living in Lutum.

And now... I was threatening to kill a man at gunpoint.

Even though not much time had passed since then, I felt like a completely different person.

Maybe I was a different person now.

I was no longer an innocent child. I wouldn't allow anyone to abuse me or lie to me anymore.

I'd learned to fight.

"Please!" he shrieked again.

I thought back to Elias's tactic inside Fort Denton when he negotiated with the Woodfaces. He'd counted down, threatening to take action once he finished counting, and it had worked very well.

"I'm giving you five seconds to give me a name," I said. "And if you lie to me, I'll know."

I wouldn't know—I wasn't very good at spotting lies, but I wanted him to think I was.

"Five," I said.

"No, please!"

"Four."

He waved his arms over his head and sealed his eyes so tightly that a bunch of wrinkles spread to his temples.

"Three."

"I don't want to die!"

"Two."

"Okay, okay, wait!" He waved wildly again and popped one eye open. "I... I just want to know what you're going to do," he said.

When I didn't answer, he added, "To the guy... I mean, the guy in charge. Are you going to kill him?"

His asking me made me think he *wanted* me to kill him.

It also made me realize that in his eyes, I was easily capable of killing someone.

Splashing blood and screams of agony flashed in my mind.

The war in Ortus.

Then, the Woodface attack inside Lockridge's courtyard.

I blinked hard, wishing those thoughts away.

I was still processing what had happened—all the lives I'd taken. Everything had happened so fast that I'd barely felt in control during the attacks. It was almost as if I'd been outside my body, watching everything. Or, as if I'd turned into an animal, and the only thing I could think of was to kill the enemy unless I wanted to end up dead.

But to kill someone who wasn't even fighting?

Was I capable of that?

I didn't want to be.

I wasn't a killer.

Or... maybe I was.

More blood flashed in my mind. The imagery was so vivid that I had to blink repeatedly to eliminate the red splashes in my line of sight. Then, I was brought back to the rover near the river, where I hid in the grass with my loaded crossbow.

The man hadn't seen me.

He hadn't known I was there, and then, with a shot through his back, his life was gone.

I swallowed hard.

"Hello?" Krampus said in a small voice.

"What?" I snapped.

His fingers curled under his chin. "Um… What will you do… to him? To the guy?"

I shook my head, still seeing blotches of red. "I-I don't know," I said. "I'll let Ari decide what to do with him."

"O-okay," he said. "I'll tell you."

I waited, my empty gun pointed at Krampus's face.

He stared at the barrel, then up at me like I was some dangerous monster.

It made me feel awful, but at the same time, he *needed* to be scared. I needed Krampus to tell me what he knew.

"Tell me," I growled.

He licked his lips and nodded fast. "It's Nestor."

CHAPTER 25

My mouth went dry.

Nestor? The same Nestor that Samesh—the dying man—had spoken about?

I must have made a face. Krampus shrieked and lowered himself into the grass. "I'm not lying! It's the truth!"

I lowered my gun. "I believe you."

Slowly, he got back up, huffing as he used his right knee for support.

Behind me, James and Dax looked about as mortified as I felt. No way could Krampus be lying. Samesh had told us who Nestor was—the very man who had robbed us at gunpoint during our migration.

How could Ari possibly fight someone like that? Her people were armed with wooden spears and weapons carved of bone. No way could she take a stand against someone like Nestor.

"What now?" Dax asked, her arms still

tightly crossed over her chest.

Ahead of me, Krampus forced his thin lips into an unpleasantly awkward smile. It was almost like he thought that if he smiled enough, he'd convince me of his innocence in all of this—that he was a *good guy* and never meant to hurt anyone.

But I'd seen the way he had interacted with Ari.

He had *enjoyed* threatening her. Maybe it had made him feel important, something he'd never felt before.

"Now, tell us about the wall," I said.

It seemed to take him a moment to comprehend what I was talking about. Squinting with one eye, he stood in silence, thinking. Then, when it hit him, his eyes ballooned like those of a frog. "Oh, the wall! The wall... yes, the wall."

Why was he saying the word *wall* so much? Was he nervous about something? Had he lied about *that*, too? Because that was the threat he'd been using against Lockridge. He'd told them that if they didn't give him food and supplies when he asked for it, he'd make it so that the ominous invisible wall came in closer, destroying their village.

It sounded like a lie to me. How could one person have that sort of power? Besides, could the wall even move?

"Well?" I said, taking a step toward him.

He raised two little hands next to his plump face. "Yes, yes, I'll tell you." Then, he straightened like a puppet being pulled by a string and fixed his blue jacket. "It was a... *half-truth*."

"A half lie, then," I said coldly.

He fidgeted with his stumps for thumbs. Then, he flashed me one of his big, oversized grins. "Semantics."

I didn't bother asking him what that meant. Maybe if I stared at him long enough, he'd start rambling again, afraid that I might shoot him.

"Well, I think, anyway," he said. When I still didn't speak, he kept going. "I mean, I have no control over the thing." He flicked his wrist and laughed as if the whole Lockridge situation were nothing but a misunderstanding. "Nestor told me to use that as a threat. I mean, I've never seen it happen. I'm not even sure that he has, either. But he said the threat would work."

"So you've seen other sides of this wall?" I asked.

He shook his head. "No... no... I've never traveled that far. The only wall I've seen is the shimmer over Lockridge's lake. And even then, I mean, come on. An invisible wall?" he scoffed. "It's probably a trick of the eye."

"It's real," James said sternly.

Krampus sucked in a sharp breath and froze. At first, he looked afraid, but it wasn't very long before his arrogance returned. He gave James an *and-you-are?* look, reminding me of the Defenders in Lutum.

"We crashed into it," James clarified.

It was evident that Dax was doing her best to keep up with the facts. She chewed her bottom lip and shifted her focus from one of us to the next. The whole thing probably sounded like insanity to her. An invisible wall? It even sounded a little cuckoo to me, as Grandma used to say.

I'd explain everything to Dax later.

Krampus pulled his face back and several rolls formed under his stubbly chin. "What? How? What are you even talking about?"

"With the rover," James said. "We crashed into nothing in the middle of a field."

Dax looked more worried now as she chewed away fiercely. "Do we think that wall belongs to the Elites?"

I nodded. "Who else would own something like that?"

She shrugged. "Anything's possible at this point."

She wasn't wrong. I'd never given much thought to the wall belonging to someone else. Not that it mattered. The only thing that mattered right now was clearing the air with Ari and figuring out what we would do about Nestor.

Throwing my chin out at Krampus, I said, "Where were you headed before your bus broke down?"

Krampus hesitated, but he started rambling when I raised my gun slightly. "Oh, you know... A few runs. For, um, Nestor. Just... Just doing my job."

"Well, you aren't doing that job anymore," I said. "It's over."

His reddish-brown eyebrows went up. "Over? What do you mean? I can't stop supplying Nestor—"

"Yeah, you can," James said.

Krampus's undefined jaw hung loose. "He'll kill me! Have you lost your mind?" He balled his fists next to his dark red face and stepped toward James.

James did the same thing to him, clearly unafraid of the threat. It was almost like he wanted Krampus to try something so he'd have a reason to hit him.

But Krampus knew better. When I flashed him my gun, he cleared his throat. "I, um... I'm sure we can come to some sort of understanding."

"Yeah, we can," I said. "You're coming with us to Lockridge to apologize and to explain everything. Ari can decide what to do to you from there. So don't worry, you probably won't be returning to Nestor, anyway."

It looked like Krampus was about to huff and stomp his feet, but he didn't. Instead, he stood quietly, inspecting all of us with his beady eyes.

"What about my bus?" he said. "I can't very well leave it here."

"Why not?" I asked. "Maybe that way, Nestor will think you're dead."

"It's a bus!" Krampus shouted. "Have you seen any other buses around here? No! Because this is the only one for miles. It's my baby, and I'm not leaving without it."

I was prepared to comment on how childish he was being when James cut in. "Well, he's right. I've never seen one in my life, so it would be a waste to leave it behind."

Before I could argue, James rolled up his sleeves. "It looks like your engine is overheating. Mind if I take a look?"

Krampus didn't seem to trust him, but what choice did he have? He didn't know how to fix his own vehicle. James, on the other hand, had experience with machinery.

"Can I come?" Dax asked, bouncing with excitement.

James smirked at her and threw his head sideways as if to say, *Follow me.*

CHAPTER 26

Krampus moved toward the rover's back door with a slouched posture, his head lower than usual.

Although I had considered tying his wrists together, it didn't seem necessary. He was afraid of James and very afraid of me and my gun. He wouldn't be stupid enough to try anything.

Behind us, Dax honked the bus's horn and waved through the window as I untied Beauty from the rover's mirror. Even from this distance, I could see her big grin. She was loving this. I imagined that driving a bus was something she never thought she'd ever get to experience. I hadn't even known what a bus was until recently.

"She better be careful with my bus," Krampus grumbled.

"You gave her proper instructions, didn't you?" I asked, sticking my foot into the saddle's rusted stirrup.

"Yeah, but she has no experience," Krampus said. "I think it was a bit reckless of you guys to—"

"No one cares what you think," James said, giving Krampus a shove inside the rover.

Krampus stumbled and landed in the back seat.

"It can't be that hard to drive straight," I said.

James smirked but didn't say anything. It made me wonder if driving a bus was a bit more complex than driving his rover. Or, was it easier? I hadn't paid much attention to Krampus's instructions. Dax, on the other hand, had asked almost a hundred questions, wanting to understand every little button and switch.

I still didn't understand what James had done to fix the vehicle—something about cleaning off residue and overheating—but it had worked. At least, for now.

"Will I get my bus back after all of this?" Krampus asked.

I almost told him he was crazy if he thought we'd give him back his bus and set him free, but instead, I kept quiet. It wasn't up to me to decide what to do with him.

Not that it mattered anyway. James slammed the door shut, and Krampus disappeared behind the tinted windows.

With Dax's loud rumble behind us, we

crossed the field and made our way toward Lockridge's crooked sign. Cool shade slipped over Beauty and me as we entered the forest and approached the black, rusted gates that separated us from Lockridge.

I sat quietly behind the rover, petting Beauty as she stomped her right hoof into the dirt. She probably didn't much like being in a forest; if I had been a horse, I wouldn't have much appreciated the orchestra of birds overhead, the thousands of rustling leaves, and the humming sound of insects vibrating off countless branches. But then again, I knew nothing about what horses liked. For all I knew, these sounds may have been more pleasant to a horse than the chatter of countless people inside of Ortus.

Beauty's ears twirled in a specific direction every few seconds, and she snapped her head sideways to follow the sound. And every time, I corrected her by trying to keep her head straight.

"It's okay," I whispered, patting her.

At the same time, a far-reaching voice echoed all around us. "State your business."

Before James could lower his window, I moved next to the rover and shouted back, "We're here to see Ari and Logan. Our friend is here. Westin."

Two people dressed in green-and-brown clothing slid out from behind the trees. Their limbs, wrapped in thin twigs and leaves, made them look like they were part of the forest. I didn't expect them to make eye contact—they hadn't last time.

Instead, they moved quietly toward the gate as bits of mud crumbled off their skin.

At the sight of them, Beauty took several steps back and neighed.

"It's okay," I reassured her.

When the gates opened, I thanked the strange forest guards and led James and Dax into Lockridge.

As we moved toward the brighter opening, I couldn't help but wonder if the guards thought Krampus was driving the bus or if they had spotted Dax behind the wheel.

It didn't matter.

Ari would soon know the truth and realize the bus was no longer a threat.

Over the lake sat a cloudy sky, which made the water look gray and cold. Throughout the village, Lockridge's bright, colorful homes brought life to the village, especially on a day like this.

But then my focus shifted to a crowd that had formed near the docks.

What were they doing?

Fishing?

Ari's dark, slender figure suddenly appeared from out of a house. She walked toward us with her arms relaxed and her bone spear at her side, swaying with her movements. Bloodred markings sat on her chin, and across her eyes was the same white chalk she'd worn last time. Her hair was the same length as it had been last time—short, almost shaved—and was still as blond as ever.

"Silver of Lutum," she said, smirking.

When I'd first met Ari, she'd barely smiled. Instead, she'd watched me with those piercing dark eyes surrounded in white, making me want to retreat into myself.

Although petite in size, there was a reason Ari was the leader of Lockridge.

She was bold, fearless, and knew how to take care of her people.

I smiled back. "Ari."

But right as her name came out of my mouth, she stiffened and jabbed the bottom of her spear into the dirt. Her cold gaze landed on me, then on the bus.

"You brought him here?" she asked in a threatening tone.

Her tone told me she thought I was working with Krampus—that we were a team, and I had betrayed her. But that couldn't have been further from the truth.

"He isn't driving the bus," I said quickly. I didn't want to allow her to start creating scenarios in her mind. "Dax is."

"Dax?" she said, tightening her lips.

"A friend," I said. "Krampus is a fake."

The hateful look on her face transformed into puzzlement.

"He doesn't have an army," I said.

It was obvious that my words were only causing her more confusion.

I signaled James to come out with Krampus, and he did, pulling our enemy by his bright blue jacket. Krampus stumbled in the sand, his arms flailing, then readjusted his clothing. When he saw Ari, he offered her the same forced grin he had given me earlier.

"Ari, my old friend," he said.

Ari didn't look impressed. I feared she might even kick him in the face.

Dax then came out through the bus's side door and gave Ari an awkward wave of the hand. "H-hi there. I'm Dax." She touched her chest. "You must be Ari. I'm not with this guy." She stuck a thumb out at Krampus. "Only driving the bus."

Ari craned her neck to search the back of the bus as if she was expecting a bunch of armed men to come out and attack her village.

Dax stuck a finger in the air, her eyes popping. "Oh!"

It wasn't like her to be so animated. She disappeared back into the bus, then came back out with a few dummy remains. As she came rushing toward us, fluff fell out of the dummy's neck and into the sand. The fluff tumbled over Ari's sandaled feet when a gentle breeze swept by.

She frowned so prominently that little cracks formed in the white paint across her eyes. Had the breeze frozen her face over? Why wasn't she moving?

"See?" Dax said, shaking the dummy until more fluff came out. "All fake. He even has a radio in there with recorded voices."

It took a few minutes before Ari's face softened again.

"You're..." She paused, then gripped her hips. "You're telling me...."

Poor Ari.

She must have felt so humiliated.

Behind her, several of her people approached with spears in hand and markings on their faces. They walked cautiously with slumped shoulders, inspecting the fake dummy, the bus, and Krampus.

"It's okay," Ari said, gesturing at them.

They lowered their weapons and stood quietly.

Slowly, Ari approached Dax.

"May I?" she asked.

Nodding, Dax handed her the limp doll.

Ari grabbed it delicately, feeling its plush body. Then, her forehead wrinkled, and fury flashed on her face. "You lied to us," she said.

Krampus twirled a finger in the air and let out a chuckle. "Oh, I think *lied* is a strong word. There may have been a bit of exaggeration—"

"You lied!" she shouted.

Her people regripped their spears, prepared to attack.

Krampus let out a little squeal and took a step back, his shoe's heel digging into the sand.

"I can explain everything if you'd like," I said.

Ari didn't speak for a moment. Instead, she stood quietly, breathing hard through flared nostrils like she was preparing to jump at Krampus and strangle him to death.

Krampus must have felt it. He took another step back, slowly making his way toward the bus.

What was he planning on doing? Running into it and locking the doors?

"Don't even try," I said coldly.

Krampus stopped in his tracks.

"And you—" Ari said, her gaze shifting onto Dax. "Who are you?"

Dax licked her dry lips. She'd already introduced herself, but it was apparent that Ari wanted more information.

"Um, Dax, ma'am," she said. "I'm... I'm a friend of Silver's."

"We met in Olympus," I said.

Ari seemed surprised to hear this. "Are you an Elite?"

"N-no, not at all," Dax said. "I'm from Lutum, like Silver."

Finally, Ari's features relaxed, and she

nodded at Dax. "A friend of Silver's is a friend of mine."

Dax seemed to relax, too.

Ari clicked her fingers and pointed at Krampus. "Take him to the cage."

Cage? Why did Ari have a cage here in Lockridge? Was it some form of prison for people who misbehaved? She seemed like such a strong leader. It was difficult to think that anyone in this village would do anything to end up in a cage.

Ari turned, leading us into Lockridge. "It seems we have much to talk about, Silver of Lutum."

As we entered deeper into the village, Logan came out to greet us, raising a brow at Krampus as Ari's people walked with him, spears aimed at his chest and back. Still, Logan didn't stop to ask any questions. Instead, he walked toward us, his bare feet kicking sand up toward his shins. He looked at peace here, in Lockridge, and nothing like the man who had been tied next to his family only days ago. Even his clothes were different. Like most people in Lockridge, Logan wore beige clothing that seemed made of the same material others were using to catch fish near the docks, only thicker.

He ran a hand through his short, gray beard and smiled at me.

When he reached Ari's side, he wasn't much taller than her despite being three times her size in muscle.

"Silver," he said as if we'd known each other for years.

I extended my hand as I had been taught to do—a polite gesture. But instead of grabbing it, he wrapped his arms around me and hugged me. I stiffened, not quite knowing how to respond. Next to me, Dax smirked.

"There's no need for shyness," he said. "You're the reason my entire family and I are alive, and I think that warrants a hug. Don't you?"

He let out an explosive laugh and patted me on the shoulder.

I couldn't help but smile.

There was something so loving about Logan—something I hadn't seen the day I met him. This wasn't surprising, given the circumstances. Jared had tied him and his family up and lit their home on fire, leaving them for dead.

He grinned at us, little wrinkles forming around his eyes. "I'm so glad you made it back. We caught some—" But then he froze and blinked twice. "Is that *Beauty*?"

I turned sideways to look at Beauty, who stood quietly next to me.

Before I could answer, his mouth went slack, and he said, "How... How did you bring her here? You couldn't have possibly walked—"

"I rode her," I said.

He ran a hand through his short, light brown hair, then brought it down over his mouth as if trying to contain many words.

Why was he so surprised?

Was it because she was so difficult to ride?

"We've never been able to ride her," he said. "The kids refused to let me give her away—"

"We would have taken her," Ari said, smirking at Logan.

"I-I can't believe it," he said.

I stared into Beauty's big honey-brown eyes. She made me feel safe, even though I could tell she was afraid. I had a feeling I made her feel the same way.

"Well, she's yours if you want her," Logan said.

"Oh... No, I couldn't—" I started.

"Westin!" James shouted next to me.

Beauty jumped back several feet at the sound of his voice. I glared at James as I fought to hold her still. Despite my irritation, Logan laughed.

Westin came from Lockridge's medical hut with a wooden walking device, a bandaged leg, and a limp in his step. I'd seen that device in Ortus before... A *crutch*, it was called. He smiled from ear to ear, revealing big white teeth that looked extra bright next to his dark skin.

"James!" Westin shouted back. He tried to walk fast, jabbing his crutch into the sand with every step, but his movements were jagged and unnatural.

"Who's that?" Dax asked.

"A friend," I said simply.

I felt happy and relieved to see Westin doing so well. I couldn't even imagine how much pain a bullet through his leg had caused, and it made me weak in the knees to think about it.

"We expect a full recovery," Ari said. "Sarmina managed to close the wound and prevent infection."

Sarmina, I remembered. Their doctor.

"Of course, it will still need to be monitored," Ari continued. "Do you have a doctor where you are?"

I nodded. We had several, but I didn't want to get into details.

"Come," Ari said. "Rest. Eat. Enjoy the beautiful weather." She smirked up at the swollen clouds above, and I couldn't tell if she was trying to be funny or if she enjoyed cloudy weather.

When Logan let out a deep laugh, I realized it had been a joke.

"Wait," I said.

Ari stared at me.

"I-I wanted to ask for your help."

She didn't respond and gripped her spear in front of her flat belly, allowing it to float horizontally.

230

"I... we..." I tried.

"A friend of ours is missing," Dax said.

I cleared my throat. "We were attacked from the other side of the river, and—"

Ari's eyes went big. "Were you followed?"

I shook my head. "No. No, of course not. We drove away in the rover. And the ones who crossed over the river—" I paused, remembering the man I'd killed.

The others had tried to chase us, but we'd lost them early on.

"We took care of them," James said, walking back toward us with Westin at his side. "There's nothing to worry about here. The only worry we have right now is finding Sadie. They shot at her while we were crossing the river, and she fell in."

Ari rubbed at her small, pointed chin, then parted her lips. She was obviously trying to piece everything together, especially the part about us finding Krampus.

She shook her head. "Will you at least sit with me for a moment? I would appreciate a more detailed explanation."

I looked at James, then at the sky, which was getting darker by the minute. Although all I wanted to do was run back into the forest and start searching for Sadie, Ari deserved to hear everything.

"I'll explain everything," I said, "but I have to go look for my friend. I was going to ask for another horse because if my friend is injured, we'll need medical—"

Ari grabbed my shoulder. "Anything you need."

CHAPTER 27

Ari nodded slowly as she shoved a few pieces of yellow fruit into her mouth. She leaned back in her lime-green wooden chair, crossed her legs, then uncrossed them. Around me were James, Westin, Logan, and Dax, all leaning forward on similar chairs.

At the center was a small matching table covered in plates of colorful fruit and pieces of cooked fish.

"I appreciate everything you have done, Silver of Lutum," she said. She was apparently trying to sort all the information I'd given her. Despite everything I'd told her—including the part about Nestor—she seemed rather calm. "Krampus will be handled. As for Nestor, there is a lot to think about."

I understood.

Nestor was a dangerous man with dangerous weapons. It would have been foolish to go after him.

"Do we think he'll come here?" Dax asked. "After you?" She looked at Ari and then at the lake. "Or... after this village?"

Ari shook her head. "I do not believe so, no. Why would he? If Krampus does not return, he will assume he was killed and will likely try to find someone else to do his bidding."

Ari and I locked eyes for a moment. Although I agreed with her, I wasn't sure Nestor would stop so easily. He had attacked us near Fort Denton, on the forest's edge.

On the other side of the river, I suddenly realized.

"What is it?" James asked.

I must have been zoned out again, lost in thought.

"Nestor," I said. "He has a way across the river."

"Why do you say that?" Ari asked.

"Because he stole a horse and a cart from us," I said. "And if Krampus was bringing him resources, it means that Nestor lives either on this side of the river or the other side. But either way, there's an access point somewhere."

"Well, whatever it is," James said, "it isn't a permanent fixture."

"A what?" I asked.

"Something permanent," James said. "We've traveled along that river countless times with our rovers. It leads to a small waterfall, but there's no bridge along the way."

"Well, there's something," I said.

Logan crossed his bulky arms and listened but didn't say anything.

"Why don't we ask Krampus?" Dax said.

As much as I wanted to ask Krampus for more information, the sun was already beginning to set, and it felt like I was running out of time to search for Sadie. Likely sensing my thoughts, Logan gave my knee a friendly tap and said, "Why don't you go look for your friend? We can manage Krampus."

James slid his sunglasses off and positioned them at the top of his head. "I'd come with you, Silver, but I'm not exactly good at horseback—"

I waved a hand to say, *You don't need to explain anything.*

"It's okay," I said. "If we don't find her tonight, we can go back tomorrow with the rover once the charge is full."

James nodded.

I turned to Dax, who stood up before I could say anything.

"Well, let's stop wasting time," she said.

"I have a cart you can use," Ari said. "For your friend."

Although I didn't want to believe that Sadie was injured enough to be carried in a cart, I had to be realistic about the situation. If she had been shot, riding a horse wouldn't be an option for her.

I gave Ari a quick bow of appreciation and followed Logan toward a small stable near the forest at the back of Lockridge. As we approached, a few chickens ran away from us, and a rooster made a loud piercing sound from somewhere hidden.

Logan placed a saddle on one of his horses—the same horse his son had been on the day of the fire. He connected a small cart that sat low to the ground. It was nothing like the carts we'd used to travel from Ortus to Fort Denton—this one was rather small, with wide gaps between the wood planks. Did they use it to transport food throughout the village? Things such as eggs, fruit, and seafood? I imagined what Sadie would look like lying on the old wooden platform. She would probably be uncomfortable.

As if reading my mind, Logan placed a worn, patchy blanket at the bottom of the small cart and patted it until it was flat. "That should help," he said, squeezing my shoulder tight. "Hopefully, she won't need it."

I nodded, fighting back tears. The last thing I wanted to think about was Sadie's dead body floating in the river. But what else could I think about? The possibility was very real.

Dax shook Logan's hand, thanking him, then said, "Yeah, Silver. She won't need it. Sadie's a fighter. If anything, she'll tell me to get off my horse and to sit in the cart."

I laughed—a sound I wasn't used to hearing come out of my mouth.

"Take good care of Fury," Logan said, patting his brown—almost black—horse.

She was quite a bit taller than Beauty, which wasn't bad given how tall Dax was.

I thanked Logan for his help, then fastened my new bow and quiver to the saddle. I was grateful to Ari for having provided us with weapons.

Then, I climbed onto Beauty and, with a kick to her sides, made my way toward the forest path. Dax followed close behind, the sound of her cart's wheels only audible when we hit rough surfaces. The rattling sound matched the speed at which she was traveling. Every time we walked through sand, however, the sound disappeared.

I didn't have to say anything when we approached the black forest gates.

The two dirt-covered guards opened them up without hesitating. Even though they didn't speak or look at me, I thanked them and said, "We'll be back in a few hours."

They didn't respond, but I didn't mind.

The moment we stepped out of the forest, Dax moved next to me and stared at the pink and yellow sky on the horizon. "Where do you want to start?"

"We should start up the river and make our way down," I said. "If she wasn't shot, she probably swam to land early on."

The thought of Sadie not being able to escape the river's current flashed through my mind. Even if she hadn't been shot, she'd received an arrow through the abdomen in Ortus weeks ago. Although the wound had closed, I knew she still felt pain; she'd often reach for her ribcage throughout the day. What if this pain got in the way?

No, *she'll be fine*, I told myself. *She's strong.*

I pushed the thought away. Unlike me, Sadie was a good swimmer; if anyone could escape the current, she could.

Dax gave me a look that meant, *Lead the way.*

So I did, moving back toward Logan's destroyed home and the river that separated us from Jared and his men. Although there was no telling how far Jared would go to track us down, I felt he was willing to take his time. At least for now, he couldn't cross any vehicle over the river, so he wouldn't follow us very far,

Maybe once his bridge was built, we'd be able to use it to return to Ortus with the rover.

Or, would it be safer to travel through Nestor's route, wherever that was? There was a lot of information we needed to get from Krampus before making any big decisions.

That would come later.

Right now, I needed to focus on finding Sadie.

I stayed vigilant as we traveled through the open field. I listened for sounds, inspected the ground for prints, and even sniffed the air for any scent that might lead me to Sadie.

Dax's voice took me by surprise, pulling me out of my thoughts. "You see anything?"

Had we already made it to the water?

Countless cattails and tall grass ran along the edge of the flowing river, and the sound of flowing water became almost hypnotizing.

"Um, no," I said, redirecting Beauty to the left.

We walked close to the edge, but only enough for me to see in the river and across.

"Sadie!" I called out.

Beside me, Dax kept her focus mainly across the river.

No doubt, she wanted to make sure we weren't being followed.

As we rode, Dax kept her fingers wrapped around an upright spear, prepared to use it if necessary.

"You think Jared backed off?" she asked.

"I do," I said. "He already lost one of his men. He isn't going to send more until he has a plan in place."

Although I hadn't spent much time in Fort Denton, I'd learned that Jared enjoyed taking his time. He'd done it with me. He'd even admitted to not wanting to kill me because he had better things planned. That meant time was on our side. At least, for now.

"He'll probably build his bridge in the coming days and then send several armed vehicles out," I said.

I thought back to the tank Elias had sent out against the Woodfaces.

A wooden bridge couldn't possibly support something that large, could it?

And would Jared go that far? Would he bring out old military vehicles?

He hadn't even wanted to fire a shot at the rover. Surely, he wouldn't risk damaging his most precious vehicles simply to intimidate us. Then again, there was no telling what Jared would do. The man was unpredictable, and whatever he planned wouldn't end well for me.

I kept my distance from the unbuilt bridge. From our location, the wood beams looked tiny, and I preferred to keep it that way. I also knew that if Sadie were alive, she would have distanced herself from the bridge, knowing that Jared owned it.

"Let's keep moving," I said.

We traveled along the river, following its powerful flow. A noise caught my attention every few seconds, and my palms went clammy.

"Only a squirrel," Dax would say. Or, "Just the wind."

We rode for what felt like hours. Eventually, the river took a turn, and we followed its bend.

The farther we went, the thicker the forest became, and we were forced to travel alongside yet away from the river.

"Sadie!" I called out, my voice echoing around the trees.

Where was she? Would I ever find her? What if she'd swum to the other side of the river? From this distance, she wouldn't hear me.

"We can come back tomorrow," Dax said, voicing what I didn't want to hear aloud.

I didn't want to come back tomorrow. I wanted to find her tonight. But we'd already spent hours searching and found nothing—not even a footprint.

"I'm sure she's safe," Dax said.

As much as I wanted to believe her, I didn't. Her tone hadn't been convincing at all. She'd only said what I wanted to hear.

Without a word, I tugged on Beauty's reins and directed her back toward Lockridge.

When we entered the village, Ari approached us with open arms.

"Welcome back," she said, a big orange fire dancing in the distance.

Behind her, people danced while others tapped on drums, creating a rhythmic melody.

What did everyone have to be so happy

about?

"Do not give up courage, Silver of Lutum," she said, no doubt sensing my pain. "If your friend is as strong as you say she is, you will find her."

I climbed off Beauty and handed Dax the reins, then stood silently as Dax led both horses and the empty cart back to the stable.

Ari patted my shoulder, drawing my attention to her. "Won't you celebrate with us?"

"What are you celebrating?" I asked.

Her smile grew so big I barely recognized her. "Why, freedom, of course!"

Although I was happy that I'd resolved her situation with Krampus, I could only think about Sadie. I'd never had a friendship like the one I had with her. I'd never cared about anyone the way I cared about her. Why hadn't I told her how I felt? I loved her. She made me feel at home, and I'd been stupid not to say anything.

Deep down, I knew she would survive so long as she wasn't injured.

That much, I was confident about.

What ate away at me was not knowing whether or not she'd been shot. And no matter how hard I tried not to think about it, I couldn't. The idea of losing my best friend—my family— devastated me.

I wanted to dance with my new friends and

eat delicious food, but how could I do that with the horrific thoughts racing through my mind? Thoughts of Sadie bleeding to death, drowning, or shivering in the forest because I'd failed to find her in time?

"I think I'd like to rest," I said honestly.

Ari patted my shoulder again. "I understand. You have a bed waiting for you in the communal tent."

I thanked her and made my way over to the same space we'd been provided last time.

I went to bed with a sickening feeling in my gut despite the sound of people cheering, laughing, and singing in the distance.

CHAPTER 28

When morning came, I was surprised to find Dax and James loading the rover with food and weapons.

Yawning, I rubbed my eyes with the backs of my hands and approached them.

"Morning, sunshine," Dax said playfully.

She ran a hand through her wet, slick hair, the scent of lavender floating toward my nose.

"Before we go—" She stuck a finger in the air, disappeared into the back of the rover, and came back with a square bar of soap. "Ari gave us some things to keep us going for a few days, and I bathed this morning. If you wanted to clean up before we go...."

She handed me the bar of soap.

I wasn't sure if it was a kind gesture or a suggestion given that I'd been wearing the same clothes for the last three days. I glanced down at my torn pants and bloody top. Dax, on the other hand, wore clean clothes made here in Lockridge. They were beige, simple, and not

"

formfitting and looked like they easily allowed the wind to pass through.

"I left you a change of clothes near the bathing dock over there." She pointed toward the opposite end of the village and past the stable. "It's quiet and private," she said. "There's even a towel."

"And so worth it," James said, sniffing the backs of his arms.

Although I didn't want to waste any time, I stank. And if I was going to find Sadie today, I didn't want to greet her covered in blood and smelling like rot.

Grabbing the bar of soap from Dax, I said, "I'll be quick."

I passed several colorful houses and walked toward where Dax had pointed. A small dock sat above the dark water with wooden privacy walls as promised.

I made my way around the right wall and climbed a small set of stairs that led onto the dock. The village instantly disappeared, leaving me entirely alone with nothing but open water in front of me. In the middle of the pier was a square-shaped hole large enough for a body to step down into, and another set of stairs that descended into the water.

What a fantastic design, I thought.

Maybe if I managed to one day return to Ortus, I could ask Finn to implement the same thing for his people.

I stared at the vast lake, wondering what sat at the other end of it.

Was there another life out there, beyond the wall? Civilization? And if so, did these people also see a wall? Did they wonder what lay behind it? Was someone sitting miles away from me, gazing out this way and wondering the same thing as me?

I inhaled deeply, filling my nose with the smell of wet earth, fish, and seaweed.

Sadie, I remembered.

Without wasting time, I removed my clothes and began my descent into the hole in the middle of the dock. The water was cold—a shock to my body—and made me suck in more air than my lungs could handle. In Lutum, the only bathing I'd ever done involved using a rag and some water warmed by the fire.

Grandma always insisted that I brush my hair every night if I didn't want it to end up looking like most people's hair in Lutum—matted, frail, and damaged. She'd told me that in her days, people used to either bathe or shower several times per week, if not every day. That didn't make sense to me. Where did they find all the water? And how had they managed to warm up so much water for so many people? I would never understand.

I was lucky if I washed my hair once every three months and with cold water.

Grandma had often spoken about how

much she missed using shampoo, whatever that was. In Lutum, we were all provided with a small bucket of salt every year—something we were expected to manage within our household. Some people used it for cooking, but most used it for hygiene purposes.

Appreciating the scent of the lavender bar Dax had given me, I closed my eyes as I rubbed the silky block across my skin. I was freezing, but I knew that in the end, it would be worth it.

When I dunked my head in the water to wet my hair, I almost stopped breathing. The cold was both shocking to my system and oddly refreshing.

I emerged, rubbed the soap bar until it lathered in my hands, and ran it through my knotted hair. The smell was soothing.

Once I finished rinsing the silkiness off my skin, I hurried back up the slimy, underwater steps and reached for a towel that lay neatly folded atop a straw box.

Shivering, I moved as quickly as possible to wipe off any excess water from my goose-bump-covered skin. Once dry, I reached for my new set of clothes. The texture felt rough against my palm, unlike the hemp clothing offered in Ortus. But I didn't care. I was beyond grateful to have clean clothes.

I slipped into my new shirt, awkwardly forcing my arms through the uneven holes when something sparkly caught my eye.

Where had that come from?

I peered toward the horizon when another flash caught my eye—this time, not in my peripheral. The flash had been blue and had disappeared as quickly as it appeared.

What was that?

I waited until more blue flashes of light finally began flickering over the lake, across the invisible wall. The light broke apart at various points, a bit like lightning, then spread in multiple directions the way broken glass reacts when it shatters.

Was I hallucinating?

I blinked hard.

I'd never seen any light come from the wall before. Then again, it wasn't like I'd spent hours staring at the strange wall.

Maybe this occurred now and then.

Despite my inner dialogue, I wasn't convinced.

Something didn't feel right, and I sensed that the wall wasn't supposed to *behave* like that.

I quickly finished getting dressed and rushed back to Dax and James.

"Did you guys see that?" I asked.

Dax raised an eyebrow. "See what?"

I pointed toward the lake. "That blue light! It came from the wall."

James rubbed at his chin, which now had short blond stubble. "No. What light?"

Frustrated, I clasped my hips and watched the people of Lockridge. No one seemed bothered or afraid. Had no one else seen it? Or did this happen all the time?

"It looked like the wall was breaking," I said.

Dax crossed her arms. "What do you mean, breaking? How can you break something invisible?"

I scowled. "I don't know, Dax. How can something be invisible in the first place? We don't know anything about this wall."

I didn't mean to throw my frustration at her. I only wanted answers.

"Why don't you ask Ari?" Dax said. "Whatever happened... maybe it's happened before."

Sighing, I rubbed my forehead. "Yeah, you're right. But I can ask her when we get back. I've already wasted enough time."

I climbed into the rover with wet hair and a sense of dread, and Dax and James followed.

"All set?" James asked.

I didn't have to say anything for him to know I was ready.

I'd been ready since last night.

I must have given him my impatient face; he immediately stuck the key in the ignition and turned it until the engine purred. "All right. Let's do this."

Pressing down on the Go pedal, he drove us out of Lockridge. I was thankful to be in the rover rather than on the back of a horse. James drove fast—much faster than any horse could travel. And if we did find Sadie today, she wouldn't have to sit in the back of a beaten cart.

"We already searched over there," I said, pointing out through the front window. "Let's go that way." I shifted my focus toward the river's bend.

"We can't go too far," James said. "Krampus told us everything last night."

I froze. What did he mean by that? When had he spoken to Krampus?

Without turning to face me, James added, "About Nestor and his hideout."

"What about it?" I asked.

Although Dax remained silent in the back seat, she leaned forward.

"He has a hideout near the river, in the forest," James said. "Not too far from the hill, where we found Krampus."

"Not too far?" I said. "What's that supposed to mean? Did he give you an exact location? We can't stop searching for Sadie because of—"

"Yeah, we can," James said. "If we land on his territory, we won't be alive to search for Sadie."

James wasn't wrong, but this news changed everything. We'd already traveled close to the hill the day before. Now, James was telling me we couldn't travel much farther than that. What if Sadie had gone farther? Was I supposed to stop looking for her because we were afraid to run into Nestor?

I couldn't give up on her.

Not so easily.

"I'll go as far as I can," James said. "But eventually, I'll have to stop and turn around."

I swallowed hard, trying to process everything.

There had to be another way.

I had to think of something.

Suddenly, it hit me.

"I have an idea," I blurted.

What makes you think Nestor wants Fort Denton?" James asked. "And that's going a little far, don't you think? If Nestor's as dangerous as Krampus says he is, he'll slaughter innocent people inside Fort Denton. There are kids in there, Silver. Women. People who didn't ask for any of this."

"Jared started this mess," I said. I didn't want to come across as childish by blaming Jared, but it was the truth. If Jared was willing to kill us, he also had to be ready to die. My plan, however, would make it so we weren't the ones fighting the war against Jared.

"Think about it," I added. "Nestor sounds like the type of man who wants resources. He doesn't have the means to get his own food. No gardens. No hunters. So, he uses people to get what he wants. All we have to do is tell him about the bunker, about the vehicles, everything. We can make a truce. Team up with him."

"You want to team up with a man like Nestor?" James said. "A man who held all of you at gunpoint and stole from you?"

My idea sounded stupid when he worded it that way, but what other choice did we have?

James suddenly stopped the rover. "Or, we team up with Jared."

"What?" I blurted. "He wants me dead!"

"He *wanted* you dead, Silver. Because people were starting to follow you, so you were getting in the way of his plans. All Jared wants is to be in charge and to have power. He isn't the type who would search for Ortus and kill everyone inside. He gave people a choice, remember?"

"And you think Nestor *would* do that? Kill a bunch of innocent people?" I asked.

"We don't know," James said. "That's the problem. We have no idea what kind of man Nestor is."

I sighed and threw my head back against the headrest.

"Jared also used an entire army of Woodfaces to try to have us killed," I said. "So no, I think you're wrong about Jared. I think he'd do about anything to get what he wants. I also think he wanted to deliver me to the Elites himself. Maybe he made contact with them, or maybe the Woodfaces told him about me. So, for all we know, he wants to be immortal."

We sat in silence for a while until Dax cleared her throat from behind us. "Why do we need to team up with either of those monsters? I mean, why is it one or the other?"

I spun around in my seat. "What do you mean?"

"Didn't Krampus say he's been stealing from other villages?" she asked. "That means there are other people out there, like us. People who have suffered because of Nestor. Maybe if we tell them the truth, they'll help us."

I stared at Dax and then at James.

Although the idea was good, the last thing I wanted was to involve innocent villages. If we asked others to stand up to Nestor, there was a good chance he'd simply slaughter them. If Krampus was taking from other villages, it meant that they were allowing him to take— that they didn't have the means to fight back or defend themselves.

"I know what you're thinking," Dax said. "That these people probably aren't fighters if they let Krampus take from them. I've been thinking that, too. But Krampus hasn't been threatening with violence. From what we were told last night, Krampus uses the threat of the wall, which is something no one knows how to fight against."

"There's no wall out this way," I said. "How could he possibly be using that—"

"I know," Dax said. "I mean... I don't know.

Maybe he uses different threats for different villages. I'm only saying that there are other options."

I parted my lips even though I wasn't sure how to respond. Then, from the corner of my eye came a figure. At first, I thought this person was a friend by the way he was moving. He smiled from ear to ear and threw both arms out as if welcoming us home from a long journey.

Dax's eyes widened. "What the—"

The man came out of the forest one slow step at a time. He bowed his head like he was laughing at a funny joke, then shook it slowly from side to side. When he reached the front of the rover, he placed two hands on his hips and watched us.

"Um... Who is that?" James asked, his hand hovering over the gear shifter stick, or whatever it was called.

I leaned forward, squinting.

The man was of average height and build. His nose, large and round, looked even bigger underneath his small, narrowed eyes. Large scars ran across his honey-beige skin—some across his neck and many over his hands and knuckles.

He wore a white, bloodstained shirt with a black, leather-looking vest over it. I'd never seen anything like that before. Across stone-gray pants were numerous tears. The skin underneath was undamaged, so I imagined the holes had come from previous attacks.

I stared at his sharp-featured face, trying to remember where I'd seen him before.

I knew this man. I'd seen him before.

He pointed at James through the rover's window, then threw his thumb sideways as if to say, *You, get out.*

James gripped the steering wheel, prepared to take off.

But it was like this man knew what James was planning to do. Still smiling, he wiggled a finger to gesture, No, *don't even think about it.*

It wasn't until another man came out of the forest carrying a large metallic gun that I realized who this man was.

Nestor.

He'd been the one to steal from us on our way to Fort Denton.

The only thing missing was a gun in his grasp.

Several more men came out of the forest with ugly smirks on their faces. It was a proud look that translated to, We *caught you.*

Nestor gestured at James again, ordering him out of the rover.

But James refused.

Instead, he clenched his teeth until his jaw muscles popped. He didn't know what to do, and neither did I. If we tried to speed off, there was a good chance they'd fire over a hundred bullets at us. But everything was over if we stepped out of the vehicle.

Nestor would probably kill us and take the rover.

But then, two more figures came out of the forest. Unlike the first armed people to make their presence known, these two came out at a much different pace.

The one at the back—a large man with a stick for a weapon—moved slowly and threateningly.

The woman at the front kept stumbling every time the man poked her in the ribs with his stick.

The woman swung around fast, her long brown hair sweeping through the air as she balled a fist at the man.

She shouted something, though I didn't hear from inside the rover.

Not that it mattered.

I didn't need to hear her voice to know it was her.

Sadie.

Insulted by her threat, the man grabbed her aggressively and shoved a rag in her mouth. Before she could take a swing at him, he grabbed her tight by the wrists and forced them behind her back.

Nestor laughed as if the whole thing were nothing more than a puppet show.

It wasn't until Sadie was forced to look straight ahead that she saw us and the rover.

Instantly, she stopped trying to fight.

Still smirking, Nestor wiggled at us, only this time, it had meant something different—*open your window.*

James lowered the window by only a tiny crack.

"I was hoping you might all know each other," Nestor said.

I considered lying and telling Nestor we didn't know this woman, but I could tell he knew better. And if we tried to lie about it now, there was no telling what he might do.

Would he kill her simply to prove a point? To prove I was lying?

I swallowed hard at the thought. There was no escaping this. We had to get out. Without a word, I reached for the handle and opened the door. Nestor's smile widened on his hairless face as I stepped out. Sadie started fighting her captor again, kicking and screaming through the rag in her mouth.

Placing a hand behind his back, Nestor paced back and forth. "Sisters? Best friends? Dare I say, lovers?"

Sadie struck her heel backward, smashing her captor right in the shin. He let out a wail and reached for his leg. It did nothing but upset him. He shook Sadie hard. "Do that again, little girl, and you're losin' a finger."

He grimaced at her, baring a set of partial teeth. The few that remained looked black and rotten and on the verge of falling out. Sadie pulled away, no doubt trying to escape his disgusting, rancid breath.

Nestor, on the other hand, seemed to be enjoying Sadie's feisty attitude.

"She's been a tough one to tame," he said, now aiming his thumb at Sadie. He laughed with a hand over his bloodstained belly, but despite the smile on his face, there was hatred behind those eyes—a look that told me he wasn't afraid to put Sadie in her place if she kept this up.

"Tell your friends to get out, too," Nestor said to me.

I peered inside the rover. The last thing I wanted was to put my friends in danger, but what choice did we have? These men had machine guns. There was no way out of this.

James and Dax stepped out slowly, and the moment they moved away from the rover, a few of Nestor's men grabbed them and pulled them away even farther.

James tried to fight back, shoving his attacker, but the red-bearded man dragging him was twice his height and seemed to have half his patience. In one quick move, he smashed James across the jaw with the back of his gun.

James's sunglasses flew off his face, and he collapsed to his knees. He reached for his face, stretched his jaw, then started searching the grass for his sunglasses.

"Don't bother," said the red-bearded man. He moved forward and crushed his boot on James's hand.

James yelped out in pain.

"Stop it!" I shouted.

Nestor's smirk flattened into a solid line, and he gave the red-bearded man a stern look that said, *That's enough.*

When the big man lifted his boot off James's hand, Nestor turned his attention to me. "I'm going to make this very simple for you." He paused, watched his men for a moment, then said, "I ask questions. You answer. Got it?"

Those cold, dark eyes of his were impossible to read.

Although most of Nestor's men had beards and long, messy hair, Nestor had no facial hair. It didn't look shaved, either. I'd seen a few men in Lutum who were unable to grow facial hair.

"It's not that complicated," he said to me, now laughing again. "Why are you just standing there? Can you not speak?"

I cleared my throat. "I can."

"Good!" Nestor shouted, his voice carrying across the field. He gestured something to a few of his men, and two of them grabbed James by the arms, exposing his belly. Dax tried to stop them, but all it took was one of Nestor's men to grab her by her short hair. She winced in pain, her contorted face aimed at the sky, then fell to the ground when the man kicked her behind her knees.

A sense of dread flooded me. What were they doing? Why were they hurting my friends?

"Who are you?" Nestor asked.

I hesitated.

Without warning, the red-bearded man smashed a fist into James's stomach.

James let out a loud grunt—the sound of all air escaping his body—then went limp. He hung awkwardly, the two men still holding on to his arms. His orange-blond hair fell over his forehead in tangles as he bowed his head, coughing.

Nestor started again. "Who. Are—"

"Silver!" I shouted. "My name is Silver."

"Silver," Nestor repeated like he didn't believe me. He rubbed his hairless square jaw and watched me curiously. "And where are you from, Silver?"

Again, I hesitated. I hadn't meant to, but I was afraid to give Nestor any information that might lead him to harm innocent people. What was I supposed to tell him? I couldn't tell him about Ortus. And although I'd considered sending him to Fort Denton, James had convinced me that I would be risking countless lives.

Before I could even part my lips, Nestor flicked his finger in the air, and James was punched in the gut again.

"Stop it!" I shouted, taking a step forward.

Suddenly, countless guns came up, their dark holes aimed at me.

"I told you the game was simple," Nestor said. "But you're making things complicated."

"I'm from Lutum," I said.

Nestor let out a laugh so loud that even his men joined in on the laughter.

"Lutum," he repeated, sounding amused. "And I'm from Olympus."

Was he truly from Olympus? The way he was laughing at me told me this was some sort of joke, and it made me feel stupid.

"She isn't lying," Dax said, kneeling on the ground.

It made me sick to see her kneeling there with a gun pressed to the back of her head. Any second now, that man could decide to end her life and blow her head into hundreds of bits.

I swallowed hard, trying to keep from vomiting.

"You're all from Lutum," Nestor said, still laughing. "I thought those people were a bunch of brainless shits. Useless slaves, lesser than scum."

I clenched my teeth. Although I didn't care to be insulted, I didn't appreciate people like Grandma being called a brainless shit or lesser than scum. The people of Lutum were precisely that—people. How could this man talk about them as if they were objects? Was this how the Elites viewed the people of Lutum?

Probably.

"Oh, don't give me that look, sweetheart," Nestor said, smirking at me. "I'm surprised you can speak, that's all. And you'll have to excuse me for not believing you. No one escapes Lutum. Your existence is nothing more than a myth across these lands."

"Well, we aren't a myth," I growled. "We're very much real."

He searched the cloudy sky with a big, ugly grin exposing the inside of his mouth. Surprisingly, his teeth weren't rotten like a few of his followers.

"You mean to tell me," he paused again, trying to hold back laughter, "that you all escaped Lutum, and you're living the good ole life out here?"

Why didn't he believe me?

Nestor wasn't a stupid man.

Maybe what he didn't believe was that we were *all* from Lutum.

"Just me," I said, then pointed at Dax. "And her."

Nestor seemed to appreciate my clarification. His face hardened, and he started pacing again with his arm behind his back like he was pondering something of great importance.

"Are you *her*?" he finally asked me.

I knew exactly what he was talking about—the Girl Who Refused Immortality.

Although everything inside me screamed to tell him he was mistaken and I had no idea what he was talking about, I couldn't. Nestor didn't seem to like lies very much and wasn't afraid to show it. If he found out I was lying, maybe Dax would be the next one to get punished. And maybe her punishment would be permanent.

"I am," I said.

Nestor slapped his hands together so hard it sounded like a gunshot. I flinched at the sound, but he didn't notice—he was too busy laughing with his men.

"Well, I'll be damned," he said. "Couple o' savages said they were comin' for you. Know anything about that? Told us before we shot 'em in the head."

"Woodfaces," I said.

"Yeah, those guys," Nestor said, wiggling a finger in the air as if talking about a bunch of ants. "You know the Immortals want you, don't you?"

I stiffened, then nodded.

"Oh, relax," he said. "I ain't about to give you to those assholes."

Assholes, I thought. I knew that word. Grandma had used it a few times when speaking about the Defenders who had abused Mother in her younger days. She'd used several other words, too, but I'd giggled at the word asshole, so it had stuck with me.

"They're greedy sons of bitches, am I right?" He aimed his question at his men, who started roaring and pumping their guns in the air. He then shook his head and continued rambling. "Wanting to live forever. What kind of sick fucks want something like that? You gotta enjoy life." His nostrils doubled in size as he sucked in the air around him. "Ya know? Appreciate what you've got because it doesn't last forever."

"And what do you have?" I asked.

His smile vanished, and he lowered his head at me, shadows spreading down his cheeks. "Excuse me?"

"What do you have?" I repeated. "What more do you want?"

He watched me carefully.

Could he sense that I knew all about Krampus? I hoped not. If he found out, he'd know that his supply of resources had been cut off as of yesterday. And if he knew that, there was no telling what he'd try to squeeze out of us.

"What kind of stupid question is that?" he asked.

"Well, you're holding us captive," I said. "Like prisoners. So what is it you want? Will you let us go after you get it?"

His frown transformed into a smile. It was

frightening how quickly his mood kept changing. He wiggled a thick finger at me, and I couldn't tell if he was about to scold me or tell me that I was funny.

"You've got balls, kid. You know that?"

What was he even talking about? I tried to keep a straight face. The less I showed what I was thinking, the more difficult this would be for him.

"For one, I want that... thing." He pointed at the rover. "And I want you to teach me how to drive it."

I glanced over at James, who looked heartbroken.

We'd come all this way to get the rover and the solar panel to keep it powered in the fields. And now, we were supposed to give that up to Nestor?

I gave James an apologetic look.

He loved that vehicle.

"And second, I want you to tell me where you two are from." He pointed at Sadie and James. There was no laughing this time or even a hint of a smile.

He was serious, which told me that if we didn't give him what he wanted, things would turn bad fast.

———

CHAPTER 30

Why would I tell you something like that?" I said.

Nestor's face twisted up, making him look like a monster. Obviously, he didn't like being talked to like that. But I'd played along with his game, and now, I felt that what I needed was to use some of Elias's techniques. In a sense, I felt like Grandma was with me—like she was giving me the strength to stand up for myself.

"Because I'll kill you all if you don't," Nestor said through clenched teeth.

"None of us want that," I said. "But we also don't want you slaughtering a bunch of innocent people." I pointed at my friends, one at a time. "There are only four of us. So if you have to kill four people so we can save hundreds of lives, I'll choose death."

Nestor looked at me as if I'd lost my mind. "Who said anything about slaughtering a bunch of people? What do you think I am? A monster?”

I shifted my gaze onto all the shiny black guns around him. “I think you’re someone who has deadly weapons and likes to take from people. I bet if you don’t get what you want, you have no problem using those weapons.”

We locked eyes for a moment. It was almost like he was fighting between agreeing with me and denying killing innocent people. If he agreed with me about killing people, he wouldn’t get what he wanted out of me. But if he denied it, he’d come across as weak.

At least, that was how I viewed it. I couldn’t know for sure what he was thinking.

“We aren’t serial killers,” Nestor snarled. “We take what we need. Nothing more.”

“And you don’t kill people?” I let out a forced laugh. “I don’t owe you any answers.”

It was obvious that my questions were making him uncomfortable. It was risky to keep pushing him, but it seemed to be working.

“Well, if you want me to give you information, I need to know that you’ll only take what you need and won’t hurt innocent people.”

He tightened his grip around his hips, digging his fingers into his torn pants.

Then, without warning, he pointed at the man behind Dax and said, “Kill the girl.”

“Wait!” I shouted.

Nestor stormed toward me and grabbed

me by the front of my shirt. "I'm not playing games, kid." His breath was hot and smelled like a mixture of sour apples and grass. "You're going to give me the information I want. Stop trying to push me."

When I didn't answer, he shook me hard. "For example, I want you to tell me where you're from. And don't say Lutum. Because you're wearing clothes that come from Lockridge."

My eyes went wide. How did he know that? Did Krampus tell him everything? Did he store all of this information in his mind? What people dressed like? What the village looked like? How large the population was?

"Tell him," came James's voice.

He stared at me with intent. It was like he was trying to send me a message, but I couldn't tell what he was trying to say. Was he encouraging me to tell Nestor about Lockridge? Or was he telling me to go ahead with my original plan about Fort Denton?

"Yeah, *Silver*," Nestor said, my name sounding fake coming out of his mouth. "Tell me."

I locked eyes with James again.

Tell me what you're thinking, I pleaded in my head.

"We're from Fort Denton," James said.

I held my breath. Why had he changed his mind? Did he know something I didn't?

Nestor scrunched his nose. "Never heard of it."

"Because it's a bunker," James said.

"You, shut up." Nestor wiggled a finger at James, and the red-bearded man shook him. Then, he looked at me. "You, keep talking."

What was James trying to do, anyway? There was something he wasn't telling me. I hadn't known James for long, but I trusted him. And if he was willing to give up Fort Denton so easily—a place he once called home—it was because he didn't think Nestor was a real threat. Either that, or he knew Jared and his soldiers could handle someone like Nestor.

I had to trust his judgment.

"It's an underground bunker," I said. "They took me in. Took *us* in," I corrected, throwing my chin out at Dax."

"A bunker?" Nestor repeated.

I nodded. "We have more of these," I said, referring to the rover.

"I knew it!" someone shouted, nudging the man next to him. "I told y'all that I saw cars drivin' around."

"So did we, dipshit," said the man next to him. "But we didn't see where they went."

"How many more?" Nestor asked.

I shrugged. "Several. I don't know the exact number."

Nestor squinted. "Why are you telling me this now? Seconds ago, you were willing to die to protect your people."

"Because I think we can help each other," I said.

Nestor laughed at me. "You. Help me?"

"Well, who else is going to help you?" I said. "Krampus won't be helping you anymore."

Nestor stormed at me again, his big black boots tearing through the grass. "What the hell do you know about Krampus?"

"We caught him in his lies," I said. Before he could cut me off, I talked fast. "His bus broke down. James here fixed it. Now, we have him somewhere secure. That information doesn't matter. What matters is that you lost your access to resources. So, you need us."

Nestor curled his upper lip over his teeth but didn't have the time to say anything.

"Our leader inside the bunker is a bad man," I said. "He tried to have me killed. He almost killed an innocent family. That's how we landed in Lockridge. Through that family."

Nestor looked so confused now that he took a step back and listened.

"The man leading Fort Denton is named Jared," I continued. "He kicked out half of his people, including us, and now rules over the bunker. He also teamed up with the Woodfaces. I don't know why. Maybe to have me and my people killed. Or, maybe he wanted to deliver me to Olympus, hoping to receive a prize. Or maybe he wanted the serum, like everyone else."

There was a long pause. Nestor didn't say anything for a while. Finally, he crossed his arms and said, "You didn't answer my question. Why didn't you lead with all of this? Why are you spilling everything now?"

"Because my friend doesn't have bruises," I said, pointing at Sadie. "It doesn't look like you hurt her." I paused. "Did you?"

"I don't hit women," Nestor said calmly.

"Jared has no problem hurting women," I said. "I don't trust you, and I still think you're a bad man. But I think Jared is worse."

Nestor smiled—this time, a genuine grin that nearly caused his eyes to disappear.

"All right," he said. "I'll play along."

"I want you to promise me that you won't hurt anyone in the bunker," I said. "Many of the people in there are innocent. They tend to gardens and livestock and raise children."

"Are they armed?" Nestor asked.

"Not the people," I said. "Only Jared and his soldiers."

"With what?" he asked.

I looked over at James, who answered for me, "Handguns, automatic rifles, grenades, and military vehicles."

Nestor sucked in a lungful of air, then breathed out slowly in a whistle. Finally, he said, "We won't harm anyone who doesn't attack us. Women and children will be untouched. That, I can promise you.”

I glanced sideways at James.

Was I making a mistake?

What if Nestor was lying?

Although this was a huge risk, I reminded myself that Nestor had used a man in a bus with a fake threat for a long time to gather resources. If he were evil, why not attack villages with his machine guns? No one was killed even when he'd held us at gunpoint and stolen from us. Not a single person.

“I want another promise,” I said.

Nestor smirked, amused by my boldness.

“You need to stop stealing from villages around here.”

He stared at me, thinking it over. “You say the bunker has its own food supply? Gardeners? Livestock?”

“Yes.”

He stuck his hand out at me. What did he want? For me to shake it? When I didn't move, he made his eyes go big and shook his hand in the air.

I grabbed it.

His grip was tight—almost painful.

“Deal,” he said.

CHAPTER 31

James sat quietly behind the wheel, glancing back at me through the little mirror every few seconds.

On either side of me were two of Nestor's muscular men holding machine guns between their knees.

"You remember our deal," Nestor said, turning in the front seat. He wiggled a little black gadget at me. "I have assurances both ways. If you're lying, you're dying along with the rest of your people in the bunker. And if you try anything to screw me over, I'll radio my buddies and have your friends killed. Slowly."

I still couldn't tell if Nestor meant his threats. Only minutes ago, he said he wouldn't harm women.

Had that been a lie? Or were his threats lies?

What if he *was* worse than Jared?

Best-case scenario, they would both shoot each other and die.

The world would be a better place without monsters like them.

"Understood," I said.

We drove along the forest, countless trees casting long shadows across the front of the rover.

"Right here," Nestor said.

James pulled onto a small dirt path that seemed to be leading to the water. The gap across the river was narrow—so narrow that it looked like someone might be able to jump across if they had very long legs.

James parked the rover, and Nestor said, "Boys."

The two men sitting next to me stepped out of the rover and made their way over to the water. They moved slowly, their big muscular backs looking too large for their heads. They bent down near a thin, dying tree and reached underneath a pile of leaves, branches, and dirt.

Together, they extracted two long planks of wood that looked reinforced with metal.

They moved toward the river and threw the planks across, causing the opposite ends to land on the other side. Dirt blew into the air when they landed, and although I couldn't hear anything from inside the vehicle, I imagined the landing had made a loud *thump* sound.

The two thick men crouched and adjusted the planks until they appeared to be straight and snug against each other.

When they finished, they got back into the rover and slammed the doors shut at the same time.

"You're gonna want to keep your tires on the wood," Nestor said to James.

The back of James's neck was shiny with sweat. He nodded, then carefully drove the rover across the planks. I felt a dip, which made my stomach sink.

Would the wood snap? Would the metal break? How did Nestor know these planks were solid enough to hold something as big and heavy as this rover?

He seemed confident, though.

The rover's front tires finally dropped off the planks' end on the river's opposite side. The sensation had been barely noticeable—a tiny *thump* in the seat under me.

"Piece o' cake," Nestor said.

James let out a sigh.

"Stop," Nestor ordered.

James did as he was told and parked the rover again. Nestor didn't have to say anything this time around. As if having done this a thousand times, his men stepped out and removed the long, surprisingly solid planks from over the river.

Within minutes, we were back on the road, this time driving on our side of the river through the big open field. James drove fast, and the rover bounced as we drove over bumps and holes.

When we approached the bunker's secret entrance, I thought I might throw up.

We only had one chance to do this right.

And like Nestor had said—if we messed this up or caused problems for him, he wouldn't hesitate to kill us. Or worse, to kill Dax and Sadie who had stayed behind.

James slowed down as he approached the hidden garage door.

The closer we got to Fort Denton, the worse I felt.

I wanted to tell Nestor to forget the whole plan—that this was a bad idea and that we should turn around. It was too risky.

But Nestor didn't seem scared at all.

After James had convinced him that he had access to open the garage door from *inside* the rover, Nestor seemed to think that attacking Jared from the inside would be easy.

What he didn't know was that Jared was an intelligent man. He'd managed to kick his own brother out of the bunker. Why did Nestor think he was stronger than Jared and his weapons? Was it because of his machine guns? Were they *that* much more powerful than other guns?

"Go on," Nestor said. "Open it up."

James pressed the same button he'd pressed when we used to go out collecting wheat.

When nothing happened, my mouth went dry.

Nestor's features hardened. "I said open it."

James pressed the button over and over again. "It isn't working."

Nestor squeezed his fingers around the large barrel of his gun. "What do you mean it isn't working?"

"Exactly what I said," James said. "It isn't work—"

Suddenly, a static sound filled the rover.

"Rover seven, come in," came a deep, amused voice.

James froze.

"Oh, come on now," the voice continued. "Is that you, James?"

Jared.

I'd have recognized that voice anywhere.

James leaned forward and pressed a little button on his steering wheel with his thumb. While holding it down, he said, "Hi, Jared."

Jared laughed at the other end. "Have you come to apologize?"

Nestor pulled a knife out from his belt and pressed it into James's neck. "You'd better be careful," he whispered.

James pressed the button again. "I'm bringing you your rover back. But I want assurances."

Another laugh.

"Let me guess... You want us to promise not

to harm your precious little Silver." He sighed. "So cliché."

James didn't respond.

"Do you think I'm going to let you step foot inside here after what you've done?" Jared said. "We stripped your rover of its access. If you really want to stop me from hunting you all down, get the hell out of the rover and get out of my sight."

Nestor breathed out hard and tightened his grip around his knife.

"I want back in," James blurted.

Silence.

"Inside Fort Denton," James continued. "I can't survive out here, Jared. It's not for me."

Jared's silence told me he was thinking it over.

"Why would I ever trust you again?" he finally asked. "You stole my rover, and you stole our most powerful solar panel."

"But I'm bringing it all back," James said. "I can't live off crab apples."

He glanced sideways at Nestor.

Why was he talking about crab apples? We hadn't eaten any crab apples.

I kept my mouth shut.

Finally, Jared sighed. "All right. Come in."

And with that, the ground split open, revealing a deep, dark opening that led underground.

CHAPTER 32

The rover's wheels rattled over the metal ramp as we drove into the underground garage. Cool air slipped into the rover's vents, and the smell of oil and chemicals followed.

"Holy shit," Nestor said, grinning from ear to ear.

He leaned forward, eyeballing all of the vehicles sitting beneath artificial lights.

"You seein' this, boys?" he said. "And the power! They have light!"

He looked like a kid being gifted a hand-carved wooden toy.

The two men sitting next to me started moving around, looking at all the equipment and vehicles in Fort Denton's garage. The one on my right rubbed his long black and gray beard and jabbed his finger against the window at a huge green tank with a big white star at the front. "Look at that, Kree. Can you imagine what we could do with that thing?"

I didn't want to imagine it. People like *them* would use weapons like *these* to frighten villages into giving them everything they had.

They both laughed—a deep belly sound that gave me shivers.

The one on my left started coughing, releasing a foul smell, then stopped laughing.

"Get your guns ready," Nestor said seriously.

He cocked his gun by pulling hard on something, and it made a loud clicking sound.

Then, he stepped out of the rover, walked around, and grabbed James by the back of the neck. James didn't fight it. He couldn't—Nestor was twice his size.

"Grab the girl, too," Nestor said.

They pulled James and me toward the garage's back door—the one that led inside the bunker.

"I want you to tell your friend to come out here without weapons," Nestor said. "You must have some sort of radio on the wall... somewhere." His head rolled around as he searched the wall, the ceiling, and then the wall again.

When James didn't respond, Nestor hit him in the back with the bottom of his gun, and James cried out in pain.

"Go on," Nestor said.

But before James could do anything, a high-pitched hissing sound echoed all around us. I tried to turn around to hear where the sound was coming from, but the two men next to me held me still.

"What is that?" Nestor growled.

The air around us became cloudy and foggy. It was only then that I noticed a smoky substance coming out from the bottom of the walls.

"What is—" Nestor tried again, but his words didn't come out.

At least, I didn't think they did.

I couldn't be sure.

Because everything went black.

I rubbed the back of my head.

Had Nestor smashed me with the back of his gun? It sure felt like it. It was sore and tender to the touch.

What had happened?

Where was I?

Around me were dark concrete walls. Overhead was a matching ceiling with a long, rectangular, flickering light. There were no windows, so every time the light stopped working—even if only for a split second—the room went completely black.

The air felt cool and damp, which told me we were still inside the bunker.

But where?

Carefully, I stood up.

That had been a mistake.

The small, square-shaped room spun around me, and I stumbled sideways, catching myself against the cold wall. In front of me was a concrete door with that familiar black-and-yellow stripe at the bottom—the same colors I'd seen throughout most of Fort Denton when I first arrived here.

"Where am I?" I mumbled.

I wasn't even sure why I was talking to myself.

But I felt completely out of it.

What had they done to me?

Then, I remembered the smoky substance coming out through the walls.

Had that smoke caused my brain to go all fuzzy? Had it put me to sleep?

"Silver," came a sharp whisper.

I froze, my hand hovering next to my bruised head.

Had I imagined someone calling out my name?

"Silver," the voice came again.

"Who's there?" I whispered back.

Where was the voice coming from?

"It's James."

I followed the sound to a small vent in the wall. "James?"

"Yeah," he said.

His voice was clearer now.

"Where are we?" I asked.

His breath came through the vent. "Prison."

Prison? Did Fort Denton have a prison?

"Inside the bunker?" I asked.

He must have nodded; he didn't say anything.

Then, he said, "Y-yeah. Sorry. I'm a little foggy from the gas."

"Gas?" I said.

"Some sort of sleeping gas," he said. "I... I'm sorry, Silver. I had to take a risk."

What was he talking about? What risk?

"Jared and I used to have code words," he said. "It was part of my training before I started doing exterior runs. The whole crab apple thing was our code way of saying an enemy had overtaken us. It was an emergency measure we trained for. But we never used it... until today."

I couldn't speak.

What did he want me to say?

I felt betrayed. The plan had been for Nestor to attack Jared. Not for Jared to capture us and hold us captive.

"I didn't have a choice, Silver," he said, likely sensing my shock. "I didn't know my rover's connection to the garage door had been severed. It messed everything up. We were supposed to go in unseen and let Nestor and his men do their thing. But that plan failed. I had to do something."

"Why?" I said.

I wanted to say, "How could you surrender us to Jared?"

"Nestor would have killed us if I turned around, Silver," he said. "And probably Sadie and Dax, too."

I remembered Nestor's threat, but I wasn't so sure he'd meant it. He'd made it clear how he felt about harming women. Maybe we could have turned around and discussed another option. But now, we were trapped inside Fort Denton and at Jared's mercy.

Somehow, this felt worse.

I rested my head against the cool concrete, trying to organize my thoughts.

But everything was fuzzy.

Why couldn't I think properly?

When would this feeling go away?

My eyelids fluttered, and all I wanted to do was lie down and go to sleep.

"Silver," James said, his sharp voice making me jump.

"I'm here," I mumbled.

But I wasn't... not really.

I pressed my cheek against the wall, and a line of drool slipped out of my mouth.

A few minutes—that was all I needed.

I closed my eyes, and everything disappeared.

CHAPTER 33

Cold water splashed on my face, and I gasped hard, jolted from sleep.

"Well, well, well," Jared said.

He sat on a small wooden chair that I imagined he'd dragged into the room.

No one else was with him, which told me he wasn't afraid of me.

Why would he be?

I was exhausted and very small compared to him.

I didn't stand a chance.

"I have to say"—he crossed his legs and locked his fingers over his knees—"that this is the last place I expected to find you."

His beard had grown out a bit, but Jared had always been very good at keeping it clean and well-groomed. It was almost an obsession. I stared at his long legs, shiny black boots, and lanky yet defined arms beneath his typical black padded uniform.

His wet-looking hair was combed over on

one side, causing a few strands to dangle over his thick, perfectly arched eyebrows.

"Wh-what's your problem with me?" I asked.

My eyes rolled back into my head, and Jared's image became fuzzy. I blinked several times until my vision came back.

"You look tired, Silver," he said.

"And you look like a monster," I said.

Jared smirked but didn't laugh. Instead, he scratched at his short beard, watching me with his cold dark eyes. I hated the way he was looking at me. It was like he was analyzing my every facial expression.

"I think we may have started on the wrong foot," he said.

I stared at his feet. "What?"

He uncrossed his legs and leaned forward, resting his elbows on his long thighs. "You think I'm a monster."

"I do," I said.

Jared's left eye twitched, which made me think he hated how honest I was.

"I never meant for those savages to attack my people," he said, his gaze stuck on the ground. He rubbed the tips of his fingers against his thumb as if trying to rid them of grease.

Was he ashamed of what had happened? Was that even possible?

"Then what did you mean to do?" I asked.

Still weak and exhausted, I caught myself against the concrete floor before falling over.

"They were supposed to scare you into submission." He turned away, then mumbled something angrily to the wall. "We had a deal."

"You made a deal with an entire army?" I said. "What did you think was going to happen?"

"I made a deal with their leader." His voice was loud now, and he nearly stood up from the chair. But the moment he caught his emotions rising, he repositioned himself in the chair and crossed his legs again.

It was almost like he was afraid of getting too angry.

Had he done something out of anger before?

Something horrible?

"What deal?" I said.

"The Woodfaces were supposed to deliver you to the Elites."

"In exchange for what?" I said. "The Ambrosia Serum?"

Why else would anyone deliver a stranger to the Elites? It seemed like everyone envied the Elites. Everyone wanted to become immortal... everyone wanted to be given the Ambrosia Serum.

"Who said anything about an exchange?" Jared said. "Arkoo, or whatever the hell his name was, told me they had no other choice. It was either they return the girl, you, or their entire population gets obliterated."

It took me a second to understand what I was hearing.

I parted my lips, but nothing came out.

Were the Elites now resorting to destruction? If so, that meant Ortus was in danger. Why now? Were things getting worse inside Lutum? Were people taking a stand because of me? Or was it simply an empty threat? The Elites weren't known for going out and attacking others. Some people around here seemed to think the Elites were simply a myth.

It was a smart way to be.

They enjoyed their luxurious lives. If they started going around attacking people, it would only be a matter of time before people attacked back.

"You seem surprised," Jared said.

"I am," I said. "I assumed they were after me because of some promise."

I thought back to Asako in Ortus and how she'd started freaking out and breathing hard. She'd commented on the Woodfaces being innocent in all of this.

Maybe she'd been right all along.

Maybe they weren't villains but rather an innocent tribe cornered into doing something they didn't want to do. And we'd slaughtered all of them.

I glared at Jared, wanting to lunge at him and wrap my hands around his throat.

"You look upset," he said.

"I am," I growled. "You could have prevented this. You could have—"

He leaned forward so fast that his boots slapped the hard floor. With a stiff finger, he jabbed the air, pointing at me. His face went beet red, and more hair fell in front of his forehead. "Don't you fucking tell me what I could have done." He froze, sucked in a deep breath, then ran a hand through his hair, pulling the strands back into place. Exhaling, he leaned back in the chair as if nothing had happened and cleared his throat. "I may have gone about this wrong," he said, now frighteningly calm. "But I'm a man who knows what he wants."

"And what is it you want?" I asked. "Immortality? Is that why you haven't killed me? Because you want to deliver me to the Elites?"

For the first time, Jared smiled.

He had enjoyed hearing that word—immortality.

It was exactly what he wanted.

I held back a laugh. Although nothing about the situation was funny, I was in disbelief over how little this man knew.

"And you thought the Elites would give you the serum to thank you for helping the

Woodfaces hand me over to them," I said.

His lip twitched. He must have sensed how stupid I thought he was.

"They wouldn't have," I said. "You don't know the Elites. They're the type of people who force women to breed, then rip those babies out of their arms and hand them over to another family. They're the type of people who will toss you on a train and throw you off if you no longer serve them. They made a mistake with me. They should have killed me when they had the chance. And now, they're realizing their mistake, and they won't stop until they find me. They think I'm the reason that the people of Lutum have had enough. If they'd use their brains, maybe they'd understand that you can't treat people like garbage for generations and think nothing is going to happen."

I sucked in a deep breath, preparing to continue, when Jared cut me off. "Then what's your solution, Silver? You seem to have all the answers."

I stared at him.

He needed me.

He wanted me to somehow get him the serum.

That was why he hadn't killed me this whole time.

"You tried to kill my friends," I said through clenched teeth. "Why would I ever make a deal with you?"

His nostrils flared, and his face darkened again. It was like he was holding back an explosion. With tight lips and immense control over his emotions, he said, "You killed one of my men by the river. I think we're even."

When I couldn't respond, he added, "And I never intended to kill your friends. We were only trying to sever the rope to slow you down."

Was he playing games with me? I never knew what Jared was thinking. One second, he looked sincere, and the next, there was no telling what he truly felt. It was almost like he had no emotions at all aside from the anger he held back.

"I don't believe you," I said.

"Are you calling me a liar?"

"I am."

He clenched a fist, and something cracked. "We didn't know you were going to get the rover. I planned to knock one of you into the river to force you closer to the bridge so I could capture you."

"And then what?" I said. "You were going to ask me to surrender? Were you going to walk to Olympus yourself? Knock on their big fancy doors and demand some sort of prize for taking me there?"

He elevated his chin, his eyes narrowing. "Something like that."

This time, I couldn't hold back my laugh.

It came out soft but came out nonetheless.

It took Jared three deep breaths to stop himself from possibly grabbing me and pinning me against the wall. There was no telling what he truly wanted to do, but I knew he was that type of man. He'd done it to me before.

"I'm not laughing at you," I said to calm him down. "I'm sorry."

It was tough to apologize to a man who endangered so many lives. But he seemed to appreciate this. And right now, I needed to be on Jared's good side. As I'd learned from my relationship with Mother, things would only get worse for me if I angered him further.

"I want that serum, Silver," he said coldly.

He leaned forward again and locked his fingers into a fist over his knee. "How can we make that happen?"

The last thing I wanted was to help Jared, but if helping him meant helping *us*, I had to try.

"The Elites won't hand you the serum," I said.

He didn't respond, likely waiting to see what I had to offer.

"The only way you're getting your hands on that is if you take it."

Rolling his eyes, he leaned back in his chair. It was like he'd been expecting some simple and achievable plan to get his hands on that serum, and I'd offered him the impossible.

"I'm not going to sit here and lie to you about how you can get it," I said. "It might not be what you want to hear, but it's the truth."

"How could I possibly take the serum—"

"I didn't say you'd be the one to do it," I said.

We locked eyes for a moment, and finally, he understood.

"*You*?" he sneered. "How could someone like you"—he eyeballed me from head to toe as if I were a rotten piece of fruit—"possibly get the serum by force?"

I smiled. "It won't only be me."

CHAPTER 34

Jared wasn't convinced.

It was a lot to ask, after all. He needed to trust that I wouldn't go back on my promise.

This whole time, my plan hadn't changed. I wanted to free the people of Lutum. I also knew this process would involve a war against the Elites—a war I couldn't fight alone.

But since being tossed from that train, I'd made several friends—friends willing to fight against corruption. If I could convince Ari to join us, and maybe even Nestor, then our chances of winning against the Elites would be good. They would become even better if we could first free the people of Lutum. Although many of them would cower as they'd been taught to do their whole lives, many others would be willing to fight for what was right.

I didn't want anyone to get hurt, or worse, die. But if we didn't end this, people would keep living in horrible conditions—inside Lutum and

Olympus—simply to serve the Elites.

"You're asking a lot from me," Jared said.

His chair screeched against the concrete as he stood up.

He paced from side to side, his long legs sending him across the little room within seconds.

"You have nothing to lose," I said. "If I don't deliver the serum, you can kill me."

It was a risk on my part because I wasn't even sure how I'd go about getting the serum. But I had to try. Right now, this plan was the only thing keeping my friends and me alive and the only way we stood a chance against the Elites.

"Say I agree," Jared said. "I'm not risking the lives of my people to go to war for you."

"I never asked you to."

Deep down, I hoped he would, but I knew that asking Jared to fight against the Elites was too much of a demand. Jared only cared about one person—himself. He wouldn't risk his life for anyone else.

"I want two of the serums," he then said out of nowhere.

Two? What could he possibly need two for? Did he have a child on the way? A lover?

I must have looked confused because he added, "My business is my own. My demand is two."

I nodded. "Okay, two."

Jared stuck his pale hand out, and I grabbed it, my skin instantly cold in his palm.

"Deal," he said.

I sat on a cold metal bench between Jared and Nestor, feeling like a complete outsider.

The space around us was cramped, warm, and made of metal. Everything was green and gray, making me feel like I'd been transported into some sort of alien ship—something I'd read about in science fiction books.

But this was no alien ship.

It was a tank—a military tank that had once been used in the war Grandma had seen.

On my left, Jared sat quietly, scribbling something on a piece of paper laid out on a thin metal square. On my right, Nestor silently inspected the interior of the tank.

Countless straps hung from the ceiling and the walls, and buttons and wires were visible everywhere. At the front, one of Jared's men sat behind a row of computers—or maybe they were monitors. He seemed to be the one controlling the tank.

Only hours ago, I had hoped to cause Nestor and Jared to go to war against each other.

Not once had I expected the two of them to sit next to each other, making a deal.

Jared tapped his pen against his pointed chin, then continued writing.

What was he doing?

Finally, he leaned forward and cleared his throat. "These are my terms." He handed Nestor the piece of paper, his long arm stretched in front of me.

I leaned back to allow them some space.

Nestor grabbed the paper with his veiny, muscular hand and read through it.

"Mm-hmm," he mumbled. "Okay." He nodded several times like he agreed with everything. Then, he jabbed his finger on the paper. "Weekly."

"Every two weeks is fair," Jared said.

"Weekly," Nestor said sternly.

Jared sighed, took the sheet of paper back, and scribbled something else. He then handed the paper back to Nestor, who smiled, then scribbled something at the bottom of the sheet. Once he was done, it was handed over to me.

"Your turn," Nestor said, also handing me a pen.

I stared at the paper in front of me. At the top, it read "Truce Agreement."

It made me think of Finn and the Woodfaces. He'd spoken about having once had a truce with them. Had they created something similar? An agreement in writing? I supposed it made sense. That way, no one could say they were unaware of the contract.

Beneath the title, it read:

The following terms are an agreement between Jared Gray, Nestor Li, and Silverstasia Blackwood. Everyone agrees to meet these conditions. Should the agreement be broken, any member will be permitted to take any aggressive action as they see fit.

Jared Gray's promises:

- Will provide a box of basic resources (food, hygiene products, and water) on a ~~biweekly~~ weekly basis for Nestor Li (suitable for twenty people).
- Will provide one rover and two solar panels to Nestor Li.
- Will not attack or harm anyone in this agreement or their people.

Nestor Li's promises:

- Will provide ten machine guns to Jared Gray.
- Will not attack or harm anyone in this agreement or their people.

Silverstasia Blackwood's promises:

- Will provide 2 x Ambrosia Serum to Jared Gray.

"Wait," Nestor said, reaching for the agreement. He plucked it from my hands, along with the pen, and scribbled something under my list of promises.

Now, it read:

Silverstasia Blackwood's promises:
- Will provide 2 x Ambrosia Serum to Jared Gray.
- Will provide 1 x Ambrosia Serum to Nestor Li.

I cocked a brow at him. "You told me you didn't believe in living forever… That a person should appreciate life the way it is."

Nestor shrugged. "People change." He laughed and looked at Jared as if expecting him to join in on the laughter. But Jared didn't. "I never thought I'd have the opportunity," he said. "I mean, who wouldn't take it if it was handed to them?"

"I didn't," I said.

Nestor's forehead wrinkled. "Well, then something's wrong with you." Laughing again, he gave me back the agreement.

"What do I do?" I asked, staring at the sheet in front of me.

Underneath Jared and Nestor's names were little scribbles that looked a bit like their names, only very messy and hard to read.

"Sign it," Nestor said. He jabbed a finger under my name. "Right there."

"Sign it?" I said. "What does that even mean?"

Jared exhaled through his nose like he was

losing patience with my lack of experience.

"Your name, Silver. Just write it fast."

Nestor laughed again, his eyes narrowing into slits. "Little Lutum girl."

I clenched my fist around the pen, fantasizing about jabbing it into Nestor's leg. Maybe the pain would be enough to get him to stop laughing so much.

"So... only my name? Right here?" I asked.

Nestor was about to say something, but Jared cut him off, "Yes, Silver. Scribble your name. Don't overthink it."

I was surprised by how calm he was being with me. His anger had disappeared, which told me he felt in control again. Was this because of his agreement with Nestor? Was he happy about getting those machine guns? Not only that, but if all went according to plan, he'd soon stop aging.

I supposed Jared was getting everything he wanted.

I leaned forward, prepared to write my name, when I realized something.

"Go on," Jared urged.

But I wasn't ready.

"I want to add something," I said.

Nestor threw his arms out. "Really? Don't you think you have enough as it is? You and your friends get to live."

"Yeah, but we aren't the only people on this planet," I said.

Nestor scrunched his nose at me as if to say, *What's that supposed to mean?*

"What else do you want to add?" Jared asked.

His tone made me think he didn't want me adding anything else—like I didn't deserve to make any demands—but both of these men needed me if they wanted their serum. That meant I had some power in this.

"I want you both to leave Lockridge alone. And I want you"—I pointed my pen at Nestor—"to stop threatening villages and stealing from people."

For a split second, Nestor's narrowed eyes led me to think he might try to fight my terms. But to my surprise, he flicked his wrist and said, "Yeah, yeah, whatever. We won't need to do that anymore with our new weekly drops."

"Pickups," Jared said.

They stared at each other for a moment.

"Might want to clarify that," I said.

They kept staring at each other, so I went ahead and made the change under Jared's promises.

- Will provide a box of basic resources (food, hygiene products, and water) on a ~~biweekly~~ weekly basis for Nestor Li (suitable for twenty people). To be picked up by Nestor near Fort Denton.

And then, I remembered something, so I added it.

- Will allow Westin to be reunited with his father.

Nestor didn't argue, and neither did Jared.

Then, I said, "I also want you to release Krampus."

I was surprised by my own words. After everything Krampus had done, he didn't deserve his freedom. But, at the same time, Krampus was a victim of this, too. Just like the Woodfaces had been cornered into going to war, Krampus had been threatened by Nestor to steal from people.

Krampus may have enjoyed the power a bit too much, but maybe once he stopped working for Nestor, he'd become a better person.

Nestor's lip curled over his teeth. "Fine."

"And we keep the bus," I said.

"The bus?" Jared asked.

"Yeah," I said. "A big yellow bus."

Nestor shrugged like he didn't care and leaned back into the metal bench. "Fine, but you won't get very far with it. We were the ones providing the fuel for that thing."

"Where were you getting the fuel?" Jared asked, almost accusingly.

Nestor paused, likely trying to determine whether to tell Jared the truth.

"Solaris," Nestor finally said.

"Solaris?" Jared repeated.

"Old village in the south," Nestor said. "They make their own fuel with corn crops—"

"I know the process," Jared cut him off. "We do the same. But we don't have enough corn crops to produce high volumes of it. Only enough for a few basics."

Nestor didn't seem bothered. "Too bad for you," he said. "Solaris has acres of corn. They use their fuel for trade. We promise them protection in exchange for fuel."

Jared rubbed at his chin, lost in thought. Was he planning on getting in touch with these people? Fort Denton ran off solar power, as far as I knew, but something told me that having more fuel would be helpful to Jared.

"I'm not getting you fuel," Nestor said. "And I'm not ending the agreement I have with Solaris. I ain't stealing from them." He glared at me as if I'd accused him of it. "It's a fair deal. It's a trade."

"Fine," I said, fixing the agreement.

Underneath both of their names, I changed the following:

- Will not attack or harm anyone in this agreement or their people, **or Lockridge.**

Then, underneath Nestor's promises, I added the following promise:

- Will stop stealing from other villages for resources. Jared's resource boxes will be enough. Will also release Krampus and not harm him.

"Okay," Nestor said, now impatient. "Can we finish this, or what?"

I scribbled my name at the bottom of the page as they'd done. It looked horrible, but before I could think about it too much, Jared snatched the agreement from me, along with the pen, and raised the paper by the corner. Underneath were thin yellow sheets. He pulled these out and handed one to me and the other to Nestor.

They seemed to match exactly what Jared had written on the white sheet, only the text was a bit harder to read.

How was this even possible?

Nestor folded his paper and tucked it into the pocket of his leather vest.

I wasn't sure what to do with mine. It wasn't like this Lockridge outfit had any pockets. So I folded it and kept it in my palm. Seconds later, the tank came to an abrupt stop.

"Looks like we're here," Jared said.

Nestor grinned and stood up, ducking to prevent his head from hitting the metal roof. "Home sweet home."

CHAPTER 35

I don't see anything here," Jared said, climbing out of the tank.

James parked his rover next to the river. Behind him were two other rovers, and out of them came some of Jared's soldiers—uniformed men and women carrying rifles.

Next to them stood Nestor's two big men with veiny, muscular arms. Unlike when they were in James's rover, neither man had a gun anymore. Jared must have taken them.

"We have to cross," Nestor said. He pointed at the river.

"What?" Jared said. "You think we're going to cross over without our tank?"

Nestor smiled like he was having fun. "Well, yeah. The planks won't carry the tanks."

Jared pointed a gun at Nestor. "I don't think so. Get your people to cross over here, and we'll do the exchange."

For the first time, Nestor looked angry—a flash of rage flattened his features, but only for a second. He quickly forced a smile again. "Don't you trust our agreement?"

"I don't trust anything," Jared said. "Including you."

Nestor's jaw muscles bulged out.

What had he been planning? To break the agreement and kill Jared on the other side of the river? Had this been his plan all along? With their machine guns, it wasn't hard to imagine Nestor winning the war against Jared, especially if Jared didn't have his tank to protect him.

With a click of his fingers, the tank's massive gun shifted sideways until the big black hole was aimed at Nestor.

"I'm going to ask you one more time," Jared said. "Get your people over here and abandon your guns. If you try anything, I'm killing all of you."

Nestor didn't look pleased, which told me his intentions probably hadn't been good.

If he was willing to break the agreement so easily, how could I trust he'd keep any of his promises?

Nestor threw his chin out at his giant men. The moment they started moving toward the river, Jared's soldiers raised their guns at them.

"Whoa, relax," Nestor said. "We have to put the planks down."

"We aren't crossing," Jared warned.

Nestor raised two hands by his face. "No

need. I'll bring everyone over, and I'll bring you your guns."

The moment Nestor turned around and took a step toward the river, Jared called out, "You're staying here."

Nestor's back stiffened, but when he turned around, he was smiling again. "Fine."

He then pointed at his two followers and said, "Get the girls. And bring the guns."

He sounded hesitant, like he was being forced to do this. I wasn't sure why he was acting this way. Jared had promised him solar panels, a rover, and resources. What more could Nestor want?

Was it being told what to do that bothered him? Was he like Jared in the sense that he hated anyone else being in charge?

Within minutes, Nestor's giants returned, both carrying a crate filled with machine guns. Then came Dax and Sadie with rope around their wrists, and behind them, two more of Nestor's followers—one man and one woman— pushing the barrels of their guns into my friends' backs.

It made me angry, but I knew that Nestor had to take his precautions, too.

My heart thudded hard as I watched Sadie cross the wooden planks. The moment she saw me, her eyes went big, and I thought she might run my way. I hoped she wouldn't. There was no telling what Nestor might do.

Carefully, Nestor approached them, tore off the ropes, and signaled them to run along.

Dax and Sadie rushed toward me, and Sadie threw her arms around my neck.

"Silver," she breathed.

I hugged her tight, wanting to never let go. Her body was warm and comforting, and even though she smelled of sweat and filth, I didn't care.

"I thought I lost you," I said into her neck.

"Never," she said. "I'm here."

We hugged for a while longer until Nestor cleared his throat. "All right, lovebirds. Break it up. We have an exchange to finish."

Jared went on to hand Nestor the keys to one of his rovers. Suddenly, I wished I had requested to keep James's rover—the one he'd connected to the solar panel. It was the only thing that allowed us to travel long distances without having to return to Fort Denton to recharge.

"The solar panels are in the trunk," Jared said.

Nestor pointed at James's rover with the solar panel attached to the hood. Its shiny black surface reflected the sun peeking through a clump of clouds. "And how do I connect it like that?"

"You can't," Jared said. "You'd be wasting your time. That panel"—he pointed at the one attached to James's rover—"is special. It's the only one powerful enough to keep something as big as a rover charged."

Jared then gave James a nasty look that told me he was still upset by the theft.

"Then I want that rover," Nestor said.

Jared's soldiers stiffened, their guns now on Nestor.

"Wasn't negotiated in the terms," Jared said. "You get that one." He pointed at a small rover that looked beaten and scratched up.

Nestor made a sour face. He knew he couldn't argue. How could he? Nowhere in the agreement did it mention *which* rover he'd be receiving.

"Fine," Nestor grumbled. He clicked his fingers, and one of his giants moved toward the rover and started the engine. It made a soft rumbling sound—nothing as loud as Krampus's bus.

"And how am I supposed to charge it?" Nestor asked.

"You don't," Jared said. "That one's a hybrid. Since your panels won't be strong enough to power it up, you'll need to use fuel." He paused, smirking. "You reassured me you have that covered."

Nestor couldn't argue. He had admitted to having a fuel trade agreement with Solaris.

"Yeah, it's fine," Nestor said, looking unbothered. He then planted his hands on his hips and raised his chin, analyzing Jared. "Then why are you giving me panels? What's the point?"

Jared arched a brow. "I'm sure you can figure something out."

It seemed almost pointless for Jared to have included solar panels. Had it been a form of manipulation? Had Jared misled Nestor into believing he'd be able to connect them to the rover? Maybe. I couldn't see what Nestor would use the panels for. He'd survived this long without power, as far as I knew. Though, he seemed very attached to the fuel he was receiving, so I wondered what he was using it for.

"All right," Nestor said. "Let's go."

He climbed into the rover with his four people and drove over the wooden planks. When they reached the other side, Nestor got out with one of his men and dragged the planks away from the river.

My stomach sank.

I wanted to run toward him and ask him to leave them in place.

We needed to get back over the river to return to Lockridge, and that was our only way across.

But at the same time, driving directly into Nestor's territory was a risk. We had an agreement, yes, but there was no telling whether Nestor would keep his promises. The moment we traveled over, he could kill us.

He probably wouldn't, given that he wanted the Ambrosia Serum, but I couldn't take that risk.

It wasn't as if a little piece of paper and some written text had made us friends.

"You look concerned," Jared said, watching me.

Sadie glared at him, so I grabbed her hand to reassure her. As much as I hated Jared, he'd created an agreement that kept us safe... for now. And for that, I was thankful.

"We needed that to get across the river," I said.

Jared stuck his arm out and glanced down at what appeared to be a silver watch. "No, you don't."

What did he mean?

"My bridge should be completed in the next hour," he said.

Had they been working on the bridge this *whole* time? Was Jared so desperate to catch me that he'd made it his priority?

He smirked as if reading my mind. "I expected to use it for a different purpose, but things have changed."

Was that his way of saying he would let us use it?

My eyes involuntarily shifted to our rover.

"You can keep it," Jared said. "For now."

His last words came out threateningly.

"I spoke with James earlier," he said. "I

understand you have a friend in Lockridge that you'd like to retrieve."

I nodded. "That's right."

"Then do what you need to do," Jared said. "I promise to honor my side of the agreement so long as you honor yours." He pointed a threatening finger at me. "But I promise you, Silver... if you fail to keep your end of the promise, there will be consequences."

I believed him.

"I understand," I said, a fluttering feeling in my stomach.

Or, as Grandma used to say, *butterflies in the tummy*.

I couldn't fail.

I had to get Jared his serum, even if the task felt impossible. But according to the agreement, I had a year to do it. That was a long time.

Jared turned to James. "You're a smart kid. I'd very much like you to return to Fort Denton one day."

I assumed he was referring to the fact that James had not only started the rover without a key, but also connected a solar panel to generate constant power. He was definitely bright.

James didn't respond but nodded out of respect.

With Dax and Sadie by my side, I moved toward the rover, prepared to get in.

"Oh, and Silver," Jared said. "Thank your friend"—he paused, thinking something over—"Maz for me."

Maz? What did *she* have to do with this? I was surprised he'd even remembered her name.

He smiled, his short beard stretching. "For the horses."

The horses.

How had I forgotten about them? We'd left them tied in the forest with the intention of returning that same night.

"I'll be keeping them until I get my rover back," Jared said.

I didn't argue. If anything, I was relieved that he'd taken them. At least now I knew they were being cared for. Without a word, I slipped into the rover next to James and breathed out hard.

The sunlight dimmed behind the tinted windows, and for a moment, the four of us sat in silence.

I turned to look at James, then Dax, then Sadie, who sat behind me.

"You guys okay?" I asked.

They both looked as shocked as I felt.

I still couldn't believe the deal I'd just made.

"Y-yeah," Dax said. "We're okay."

"You ready to go get Westin?" I asked.

Everyone nodded.

James fixed his sunglasses. Across the right

lens was a big scratch—no doubt the result of the beating he'd received by Nestor's red-bearded follower.

"Here we go," James said, pressing down on the Go pedal.

CHAPTER 36

We zipped through the open field, passing forests and hills. Jared followed with his tank and another rover. As I stared at the clear sky, watching the several clouds float by, I wondered if we were falling into one of his traps.

But I quickly pushed those thoughts away.

Jared had seemed sincere when he said the bridge would be completed.

And what reason did he have to mess with us? He'd let us keep the rover. Why? Because he wanted that serum more than anything, and I was the only one who could get it for him.

That meant, for now, we were safe.

When we approached the bridge, several armed soldiers moved aside, pointing their guns toward the sky. Jared must have communicated with them through radio. It was like they knew we were coming.

Dozens of builders worked on the bridge, sanding down the wooden side railings. But when they saw us, they quickly stepped off to allow us passage.

James lowered his window and thanked them, and the scent of cedar swept into the rover as we drove over the new bridge.

It was slightly curved and made no sound as we drove over it.

Unlike Nestor's planks of wood, this felt very sturdy—something solid enough to handle several rovers at a time. Not that it could fit that many vehicles at once; it was still small, which was likely the only reason they'd managed to build it so fast.

After crossing, we sped through the familiar field near Logan's burned home.

By the time we reached Lockridge, the sun had begun to descend in the sky.

Ari welcomed us as she always did—with a sweet yet reserved smile.

"Silver of Lutum," she said to me, then noticed Sadie stepping out of the rover. "I am pleased to see you were successful in your search."

I introduced Sadie to her, and Ari welcomed her instantly.

"Our fishers just caught a batch of crabs," Ari said. "You must be hungry."

I appreciated how quickly Ari always offered us food. Having been raised in a place where food was so scarce, this meant a lot to me.

I thanked her for her generous offer and followed her toward the village's common area. Blue-painted wooden chairs were positioned everywhere as people gathered for their evening meal. Several fires formed a row, and atop these were metal pots bubbling with water.

From the docks came two girls dragging big nets full of dark green bugs. At least, they looked like bugs, only bigger and with strange fuzzy legs. I blinked hard, staring at the odd little creatures.

Suddenly, I had no appetite.

Did Ari really expect us to eat... *those?*

"Unlike our ancestors," Ari said, "we don't allow live cooking."

Live cooking? My eyes bulged. Was that what it sounded like? I hoped not.

Ari opened one of the nets and extracted a crab. Its little legs wiggled around as it tried to escape her. From her side, Ari extracted a short bone knife no longer than a finger. With it, she stabbed the crab somewhere in the underbelly and tossed it into one of the pots full of boiling water.

"We kill them first," she said. "And that's something I expect you to learn if you are going to be spending time here." She smirked suggestively.

Was she inviting me to stay in Lockridge?

I smiled back.

"How did our ancestors do it?" I asked, even though I wasn't so sure I wanted to know.

"They threw them in alive... into boiling water," she said. "The crabs would scratch at the sides of the pot, trying to get out."

I felt nauseous at the thought of it. "Why would they do that?"

"To kill bacteria instantly," she said. "But do a few seconds really make that much of a difference?" She showed me her little bone knife and wiggled it between her fingers. "This thing prevents a lot of suffering."

She stuck her arms out as if showing me all of Lockridge. "We honor all life here in Lockridge."

I appreciated this sensitive side of Ari.

People cheered and clapped. Ari then bowed her head, closed her eyes, and mumbled something, as did a few others. What was she doing? Praying? Although I knew about prayer, it had never been tolerated in Lutum.

After they finished their words, Ari waved her hand, gesturing at the young girls to start their cooking process.

Like her, they pulled out little bone tools and started piercing the crabs, one at a time.

I felt awful watching it, so I turned away.

Ari appeared next to me with her short arm wrapped over my shoulder. "You are a good soul, Silver."

I didn't know how to respond to that. It

seemed like a normal thing to not want animals killed or harmed in any way.

"We have a lot to talk about," I told her.

"Come," she said, leading me to a row of chairs near the water.

I sat down, and the chair sank into the sand a bit. My friends did the same, and when it was James's turn to sit down, he panicked, throwing his arms out as his butt hit the chair. It was like he thought he was going to sink into the sand completely.

Dax burst out laughing, and Sadie smiled at me.

It was nice to see everyone happy and safe.

Behind Ari and around the cooking pots were Logan and his family—his wife, his son, his daughter, and his little one crying in her mother's arms. They all waved at me, smiling. I waved back. It felt amazing.

James leaned forward, clapped his hands together with excitement, and said, "Silver, you wanna tell them?"

Everyone looked at me.

"I made an agreement with Nestor and Jared," I said.

A few gasps echoed, and several people approached. Ari, however, remained as composed as she always did. She didn't react, and instead, listened.

I told her about Sadie's capture and about how we'd fallen right into Nestor's hands. I explained everything else from that point on, offering all the details I could remember. When I wasn't sure about something, James cut in and explained his side of the story.

By the end of it, Ari looked impressed.

"I-I am at a loss for words, Silver of Lutum," she said.

A hint of a smile flashed across her face. Was it gratitude?

"You agreed to keep us safe," she said. "You owed us nothing."

"I don't do things because I owe anyone anything," I said. "It was the right thing to do."

James leaned in his chair and nudged my elbow, reminding me about our conversation from the other day—the one we'd had after he'd saved me from the river. He'd said it had simply been the right thing to do.

Ari thanked me over and over again, then said, "I can never repay you for this."

I hesitated.

There was something she *could* do, but I didn't want to make it seem like I'd protected her village only to ask her for something in return. That hadn't been my intention. But what I wanted from her was something that would save a lot of people—now and in the future.

"Something is on your mind," she said.

Dax knew what I wanted to ask. She played with her fingers without looking up at anyone.

She had come from Lutum, and like me, she wanted to put an end to the way the Elites enslaved people. Sadie didn't seem to understand as much as we did; she'd grown up in Ortus. But she also knew how much this meant to me.

"I want to free the people of Lutum," I said.

A slender man appeared next to Ari carrying a clay cup. She took it and thanked him, brought it to her lips, and took a sip. After swallowing the liquid, she let out a satisfied sigh. "What do you need from us? Resources? Weapons? Livestock?"

She wanted to help.

But I wasn't sure she was willing to go to war. No leader wanted that for their people. This was a lot to ask.

When I didn't respond, her lips tightened into a flat line. "I see."

"The Elites will never stop, Ari," Dax said.

I was surprised she dared to speak to Ari like that.

Ari observed her.

"These people are playing with lives," Dax said. "They enslave humans... beat them. Torment them." She shifted her gaze onto nothing, likely reliving certain difficult moments in Lutum or even Olympus. "And now, they're manipulating human babies. They're growing them inside some lab. They've caused all kinds of deformities."

"We think," I said.

We couldn't be sure. Although everything added up, there was no telling for sure if Dr. Bartek was the one responsible for all those awful mutations. While the people of Ortus thought Daemons to be horrible monsters, Danika had seen them with her own eyes, and she'd described them as mutated people—people who might have turned out bad because of experiments.

What kind of sick person experimented on people?

Or on anything with a heartbeat?

Dax nodded. "Well, it adds up... Anyway, all I'm saying is that the Elites are awful. They think they're gods. They won't stop until they have Silver, and once they do, there's no telling what they'll do to the rest of us."

"They threatened the Woodfaces," I said. "Told them if they didn't capture me, they'd destroy their village." I paused, inspecting the beautiful, colorful houses around me. "What if they threaten you next?"

It was apparent that Ari didn't know how to respond. She took another sip of her drink, thinking everything over.

"This is a lot," she told me. Taking another gulp, she wiped her mouth with her small fingers. "I have a proposal."

I stiffened.

"Tonight, we celebrate." She raised her cup.

"Our freedom, your freedom, and the fact that our dear friend Westin will be allowed to reunite with his father."

Logan suddenly appeared next to her and dropped a hand on her small shoulder. "What's going on here? You all look so serious. Is everything okay?"

Ari stood up, her chair barely moving in the sand. "We are free, my dear Logan." She raised her cup again. "Tonight, we celebrate!"

People cheered and threw their arms in the air.

Then, discreetly, she turned to me and said, "Let's continue our discussion tomorrow. You have all had a long day. Eat. Sing. Dance to your heart's desire!"

At once, drums started beating, and Ari swayed from side to side, carrying her drink above her head.

It was strange to see such an intimidating woman with tribal markings drop her spear and dance as if she no longer had any responsibilities.

I wished I could learn to relax the way she did.

James patted my shoulder. "She's right. Let's call this a day, forget about everything, and have a bit of fun."

Fun? What was *fun*, anyway? Dancing? How could we dance after everything—

Without warning, Sadie grabbed me by the

arm and pulled me out of my chair. With a forced smirk on her face, she said, "Hey, if I'm doing this, you're doing it, too."

I thought back to the time Lyson and I had been dancing in Fort Denton—the time we'd crashed into Jared's table. Right before the crash, however, I had been enjoying myself quite a bit. I'd given in to the music and allowed my body to move to the rhythm.

"Okay," I said, following Sadie toward the fire.

Her movements were awkward and looked unnatural like she didn't know how to dance. Maybe she didn't—she hadn't seemed very keen on dancing inside Fort Denton, so I got the feeling she was only doing this for me.

"Come on!" she shouted, now clapping her hands.

Her exquisite smile was contagious. I stared at her, wanting nothing more than to pull her in and kiss her.

Out of nowhere, James came running and threw himself onto his knees. Sand splashed everywhere, and his sunglasses flew off his face. But since the sun was setting, he didn't seem to care. Rather than put them back on, he tossed them a little bit farther—out of reach from everyone's stomping feet.

His face contorted, and for a second, I thought he was in pain. But when he started pretending to play some sort of instrument, I realized he was only being playful. He strummed something over his chest and moved his left hand's fingers wildly.

"Air guitar, baby!" he said. "Ner ner ner, ner ner!"

His voice came out high-pitched and, surprisingly, meshed well with the beat of the drums. It was so ridiculous that I burst out laughing harder than I'd ever laughed.

"Dax, drums!" he shouted, pointing at Dax.

She started hitting the air, smashing open palms into nothing, hitting a set of invisible drums.

"Silver, bass!" James shouted.

I stood, frozen. What was bass?

"N-never mind!" he said.

When Logan joined us, he said, "Logan, bass!"

Logan went on to make almost the same movements as him, only less chaotic.

I laughed some more and pinched the bridge of my nose, feeling silly and a bit embarrassed. I'd never seen anyone act so wildly before—so out of control. But I liked it. And I could tell that everyone else was enjoying it, too.

"Silver, do something!" James shouted.

He stood up now, still playing with his invisible instrument.

Awkwardly, I started drumming the way Dax was doing. I knew I probably looked stupid, but I didn't care.

"Yeahhhh," James said, nodding over and over again. "That's it!"

The more I got into it, the harder I hit. Then, I stomped my feet, moving my body to the rhythm. Real music suddenly filled the air, making me want to dance even more. Next to us were four people blowing into what looked like horns with little holes.

I'd never seen anything like it, but the sound was incredible.

We danced and danced for what felt like hours until the sun went down. And even after that, we kept dancing and singing. But the best part of my evening was when Sadie grabbed me from behind, held me tight, and kissed my neck.

"I missed you," she said.

I squeezed her forearms—my way of hugging her back. "I missed you too."

Without warning, she playfully tapped my butt the way Grandma used to do when I was young. Still, it took me by surprise, and I jumped.

She laughed. "Keep dancing!"

CHAPTER 37

When morning arrived, I didn't want to get out of bed.

Next to me, Sadie slept so deeply that she snored. It was cute, and I knew that if I told her about it later, she'd deny it and say she wasn't a snorer. She'd done it before.

Smiling, I closed my eyes again and moved closer to her.

I lay there, appreciating her heat—appreciating her.

Then, I thought of the discussion we were going to continue today. If I went to war against the Elites, Sadie would want to join. No matter what I said or how many times I'd beg her not to take part, she wouldn't listen. She'd want to fight by my side.

I felt sick to my stomach at the thought of losing her.

She had become my best friend and more—my family.

I lay in silence as countless thoughts

rushed through my mind. Eventually, my friends woke from their sleep. First, James, and then Dax. They sat upright, yawning, and James immediately reached for his sunglasses.

Sadie woke up next, groaning against me.

I hugged her tight and smiled at her.

"Morning," I said.

She pulled away from me. "You need to chew some mint, Silver."

I frowned, covered my mouth, but laughed—a muffled sound. "And you don't?"

Sadie chuckled, and Dax laughed at us.

When we exited the large hut, a few unfamiliar faces greeted us with fresh piles of clothes and towels. On top of the towels were a few bars of soap.

"A gift from Ari," said a young boy.

His golden skin was freckled and shiny. He looked shy and seemed unable to make eye contact. I thanked him and grabbed one pile. Dax grabbed the other from the young girl next to him. She looked a lot like him, so I imagined they were siblings.

Far behind them was a young couple cheering them on. Who were they? Their parents? When the children returned to them, the couple hugged them, and the man ran a hand through his boy's hair as if to say, *I'm proud of you.*

I stared at them for a moment, feeling awful.

"You can't think that way," Sadie said as if reading my mind. "You can't picture everyone here dead because of the war. We don't know what's going to happen when the time comes."

I swallowed hard. "I know."

As the sun began to rise, filling the sky with a beautiful orange glow, more and more people came out of their homes.

Sadie looked more excited than I'd ever seen her as Dax explained to her where she could bathe. She got even more excited when Dax said it was completely private. We didn't have anything like this in Ortus—only a river behind a tall, wooden fence. And with such a high population, several people often bathed at the same time.

Sadie ran off with her new clothes, towel, and bar of soap, looking like an excited child.

The rest of us sat in Lockridge's blue wooden chairs, barely talking.

"You sleep okay?" James finally asked to clear the silence.

I nodded, even though I was still tired.

Dax yawned, which told me she was, too.

"Long day yesterday," James said.

It had definitely been long. Was I still tired because of the gas? Or was I exhausted because of everything that had happened? It didn't matter. We had another long day ahead of us. But I didn't want to think about it. Right now, all I wanted was to enjoy my time here in

Lockridge.

There was something special about this place.

And now that Ari had hinted I could stay, I had a lot to think about.

I'd already told everyone in Ortus that I wouldn't be returning for their own safety.

But here, in Lockridge, I was far away from Olympus.

I hadn't seen another Eye since Ortus. Maybe the Eyes couldn't fly out this far. Or, maybe they'd given up. Was that possible? I'd know for sure once I heard from Finn. If the Elites had given up, maybe the best thing for us would be to stay hidden a bit longer before returning.

Jared had given me a year to fulfill my promise.

What if I waited a little while? What if I simply... lived?

Everyone was exhausted. We'd gone through several wars in a matter of days. Maybe what everyone needed most of all right now was time to heal and rebuild.

And, maybe there was another answer.

What if I could free the people of Lutum without leading an entire army to Olympus?

Lives could be spared.

"Silver," James said.

He shook me out of my thoughts. When I looked up at him, he grinned a set of straight teeth, waved air into his face, and inhaled deeply. "Take it all in. Enjoy this. We won't be here forever."

I hesitated.

"Right?" he said. "You're coming back to Ortus, aren't you?"

"You heard what I told everyone," I said. "I told them I was leaving."

"And you left," James said, frowning. "We made agreements. We did a lot, Silver. Why wouldn't you come back with us?"

I shrugged. "I don't think it's safe yet."

Dax didn't say anything. She sat quietly, focused on the little ripples across the lake.

"Dax," James said. "Say something."

But she couldn't. She knew as well as I did that this was the safest option for everyone. Everywhere I'd gone, destruction and death followed. Lockridge seemed the only place secluded enough to not capture the attention of the Elites.

"Ortus needs time to rebuild," I said. "If I go back, and the Elites choose to attack—" I paused, imagining Ortus blowing up in flames. "I can't put anyone else in danger."

James let out a sharp, impatient breath. "But you aren't. If we go back, and there's been no attack, then it's safe—"

I smirked. "I'll miss you too, James."

He stopped talking and blew into his cheeks. "Are you sure this is what you want?"

"I am," I said.

"Then I'm staying too," he said.

"Me too," Dax said.

My jaw went slack. "Um, no. James"—I pointed at him—"Ortus needs you. You're the only one with a rover, which means you can bring everyone wheat. And now that we have the bridge, it's going to make things a lot easier."

James opened his mouth to speak, but I cut him off. "And you." I pointed at Dax. "Mia is still in Ortus. Aren't you two together or something?"

Dax sighed at the thought of her. It was apparent she missed her.

"So, no," I said. "You both need to go back."

"And what about Sadie?" Dax asked.

I held my breath. I hoped Sadie would stay with me, but it would be up to her to make that decision.

Before I could answer, Ari walked toward us with Logan by her side. She hadn't painted her face yet, which made her look much softer and less intimidating.

She sat down without a word and gazed off into the lake. "Beautiful village we have here, wouldn't you say?"

What was she getting at? I had the feeling she didn't really want me to answer her.

"I owe you everything, Silver of Lutum." Her tone was sad. "But I cannot risk the lives of my people for a war we do not belong in."

"It's okay," I said, honestly. "It was a lot to ask."

She didn't respond.

I wondered if she felt bad for refusing to join me. I didn't want her to feel bad. What I wanted was to find a way to free the people of Lutum that didn't involve risking the lives of so many people. Maybe if I spent time here, reflecting, I'd somehow find that solution.

"I'm sorry," she finally said.

I forced a smile. "Don't be. I have a lot of thinking to do, and I hope to find a way to end all of this without too much bloodshed."

"You are very wise," Ari said. "I'm certain you will find what you seek."

I clasped my hands together, trying to figure out the best way to ask Ari to stay. Rather than think too hard, I simply asked, "Would you mind if I stayed here, in Lockridge?"

Ari's plush lips stretched into a sweet, almost childlike grin. "I would love nothing more."

She got up quickly, shook my hand, and pulled me in for a hug. Logan shook my hand next, patted me hard on the back, and welcomed me to Lockridge.

It felt... right.

Like I belonged here.

I sucked in a lungful of the fresh morning

air.

What more could I want?

I'd be among friends here, and I would be comfortable and cared for.

Although I wished all my friends could join me, this wasn't goodbye.

Now that we had access to Jared's bridge, we could easily see each other, especially since James had gotten to keep the rover. Maybe he could even bring Rose, Danika, and Asako here for a visit.

Without the risk of Nestor and his people hiding in the forest, and without the threat of Jared hunting me, everything would be okay.

Even the Woodfaces were no longer a threat.

The only danger now was the Elites.

And if I stayed out of their way, maybe everyone would be safe.

As the village thickened with bodies, Sadie made her way back to me. She looked happy with her wet hair, clean skin, and a fresh change of clothes. But the moment she joined us at the chairs, she knew something was going on.

"What?" she asked. "What's going on?"

"Silver's ditching us," James said, his brows slightly slanted.

Sadie's eyes went big, but Ari quickly said, "Silver is joining us here, in Lockridge." She paused. "And what of you, Sadie of Ortus? Will you join us, too?"

I swallowed hard, waiting.

Sadie reached for my hand and locked her fingers around mine. She didn't have to say anything for me to know her answer. With a sweet smile, she comforted me instantly.

I gave her hand a gentle squeeze to say, *Thank you.*

We stood there in silence for a while, watching the vast, open lake.

"I think this is good," I breathed.

"Me too," she said, blinking as a gust of wind swept by.

"But you know it isn't forever, right?" I said.

She turned to look at me, a knowing smile stretching her beautiful lips. "Of course, I know that, Silver. You don't give up on anything. You're stubborn. So, I know it's only a matter of time before we get back out there to save your people."

I leaned my head on her shoulder, thankful for her understanding.

Then, I thought of Grandma and my division—how the Elites had destroyed it—and a hot rage burned inside me.

"I don't only want to save my people," I said.

She stared at me.

"I want the Elites to pay for everything they've done," I said.

She stared at me intently, like she could feel my pain. "Then they will."

CHAPTER 38

For the first time, everything felt right.

Standing next to Sadie felt like home, something I wasn't so sure I'd experienced before. Even in Lutum, I'd never felt at home—instead, I was more like a prisoner. Grandma was the only home I had back then; she'd made me feel safe.

Sadie did that too.

And so did Lockridge.

It truly seemed like everyone here cared about one another—like they were willing to lend a helping hand to anyone who needed it. And I knew they were because I'd seen it. So many times, someone had come running to help someone carry a crate of fish or untangle netting from around a dog's paw.

Lockridge was a special place, and I was grateful to be there.

I leaned my head on Sadie's shoulder, wanting to thank her for everything she'd done for me. But right now, I enjoyed the silence. So I stayed quiet, appreciating all the beauty the lake had to offer—the little shiny ripples across the water, the occasional splash caused by a creature, and the faint smell of fish that made its way up my nose.

In the sky, dozens of gray-and-white birds flew in circles, cawing. Every few seconds, one of them dove straight into the water. It made me laugh. What were they doing? Swimming? It wasn't until one of them came back out with a fish dangling from its beak that I realized it was catching its food.

But then, something else caught my attention—something unrelated to the water that made my smile disappear.

On the horizon came a bright blue flash of light. It started from the top, high up, where I thought the sky ended, and broke into pieces as it came down. But it wasn't lightning. It was the same blue flash I'd seen on the invisible wall when I'd been bathing.

"Did you see that?" I asked.

Sadie blinked a few times, then squinted toward the wall. "Y-yeah," she said. "I did. Is that the invisible wall you were talking about?"

I nodded. "That's the second time I've seen it do that."

Behind us, Ari stepped toward the water, her sandaled feet inches away from a frothy wave making its way to shore. The way she watched the blue light told me this was the first time she was seeing it.

She stood with her shoulders pulled back and her hand fastened tightly around her spear.

I watched her, then the light.

"Is everything okay?" I asked.

She didn't respond, and the frightened look on her face told me everything was *not okay*.

Before anyone could speak, something else happened... something terrifying.

Where the wall met the water, bright blue now flashed wildly. Within the mixture of light came something else: a foam-like substance. It appeared to be getting larger and larger, and under the pads of my feet came a tickling vibration.

"Ari?" I asked, taking a step back.

Her eyes widened in horror.

A frightening sound echoed throughout the entire sky—like a crack of thunder, only several times louder. It shook the whole village, and bit by bit, the line of foam intensified, growing taller and taller.

Only, it wasn't foam... it was water.

I gasped. "Is that—"

"A wave," Ari said. She took several steps back, looking confused. "It's... the wall. It's moving."

As the invisible wall with blue flashes seemed to draw in closer, the wave grew in height.

"It's coming this way!" Ari suddenly shouted.

Her voice pierced through the village. "Run!"

People scrambled; others fell. For a moment, I froze, watching the wall move toward Lockridge. The wave that had formed at its base seemed to run for miles on either side. How was this even possible? How was the entire wall shifting? Would it reach land?

"Silver!"

Sadie grabbed me by the arm and tugged. I ran backward for a moment, before turning around and following Ari and the others. Logan came out of his home, carrying his little girl. He had no shoes and looked unkempt, as if he'd only now woken up. He rubbed his eyes several times, then started shouting at his family through his front door, urging them to get up.

More and more people ran from their homes, their necks twisted as they watched the horror unfold miles away on the lake's surface.

Every second, the wall drew nearer, and the wave grew taller than all of the houses.

I was surprised to see Krampus come running out, his little legs moving quickly. He stared, petrified, his jaw slack. Then, he started running toward his bus.

Where was he going? Taking off? But to my

surprise, he started shouting at people to get in.

I couldn't hear him over the eerie, sky-filling sound, but his mouth was a gaping hole. He ordered people around by jabbing his finger at them and pointing toward the bus.

Several women and children climbed on, some carrying clothes and towels, and others, nothing at all. There hadn't been enough time to grab resources.

Then, the deep sound of a horn echoed throughout the village. A man had sounded it; he stood tall and shirtless, revealing a muscular abdomen and tribal markings trailing down his dark arms.

More people came out of their homes in a panic.

Some rubbed their eyes, and others walked around, trying to ask questions.

But there was no time for that.

"Go!" I shouted at a young couple with a baby.

The young man caught a glimpse of the giant wave coming our way, then urged his partner and child toward the bus. The big yellow bus shook from side to side as people squished themselves onto it. I imagined there were far more people in there than there were seats.

Would the bus still be able to drive?

I hoped so.

Logan ran toward the stables, freeing horses and slapping them on their butts.

Dax managed to grab one and climb on it bareback.

I wanted to do the same, but I wasn't experienced enough. And there was no time to put a saddle on any of them.

Without wasting time, Krampus closed the bus's door and started driving backward through Lockridge's forest path.

"Get in!" James shouted, pointing at the rover.

But behind him was an elderly couple who could barely stand straight. The man winced and grabbed his back as he walked, and the older woman beside him tried to help him, though she looked frail.

"Take them!" I said.

James hesitated but quickly ran to grab the elderly couple. He urged them to get into the rover, then found another child and her father, and told them to get in, too.

Ari's armed fighters held on to their weapons as they ran, crowding near the forest's path.

I wanted to keep running, but when Ari froze, so did I.

She stood in disbelief as sand exploded on shore and the massive wall of water came straight for Lockridge. The water was dark, with flashes of blue light crackling through it.

The docks blew up into tiny bits as if made from nothing more than sand.

I wasn't sure what was to blame for the awful destruction—the water, the wall behind it, or both combined.

Next, homes exploded, and wood flew in every direction.

Ari slapped a hand over her mouth, in shock.

Several of her fighters tried to grab her, but she stood firmly in place.

"Silver!" Sadie shouted. "Let's go!"

She pulled on me, but I didn't follow.

I couldn't let Ari stand there and die.

I rushed in front of her, trying to block her view, but she simply stared through me.

"This isn't over!" I shouted in her face. I grabbed her small, muscular shoulders and shook her. She seemed unbothered by it. "We need you, Ari! Your people need you! I lost my entire village, too!"

Her dark eyes turned on me.

"It's only material, Ari," I said. "People are what matter!"

When she didn't respond, I shook her again.

"Silver—" Sadie said, sounding terrified.

The sound of destruction was so loud I could barely hear her voice. Chairs flew toward us while others floated in the air, stuck against the moving wall. Desks, beds, and tables crashed into the sand, shattering instantly.

It saddened me to see the colorful homes blow up—to see such a beautiful village crushed so quickly. But we couldn't stand there watching it happen. If we didn't leave, we'd die.

I shook Ari hard again. "This can be fixed. But it can't be fixed if you're dead."

Her gaze landed on me again, so I took the opportunity to give her a shove. "Let's go!"

She stumbled backward a few times, her eyes wide and terrified, then started shouting at her people. "Move! Move! Move!"

People ran as fast as they could—some with great speed, others slowly and in need of assistance. But everyone helped where they could. Some of the more muscular men scooped up older women and children and ran with them in their arms.

The guards at the gates were quick to abandon their posts. They ran with Ari and the others, aiming for the other side of the forest. For a moment, I thought the trees might protect us. They were, after all, rooted deep in the ground.

But when the sound of ripping and snapping echoed behind me, my stomach knotted.

I turned my head sideways to catch a glimpse of trees being ripped from the ground. Some split and came tumbling down, while others unrooted entirely, their massive trunks speeding toward us. Loud snapping and ripping filled the air as leaves exploded and branches flew in every direction.

A colossal wave of dirt and sand formed at the base of the wall, dragging along with it all the broken trees, pieces of beds, chairs, walls, and the remains of Lockridge that had been intact only seconds ago.

No matter how fast everyone ran, the wall seemed to be catching up.

At the back of the crowd, a man fell to his knees, and my heart almost stopped. The giant wave of water, dirt, and debris came at him fast, about to crush him.

A big man helped him up, wrapped his arm around his neck, and tried to hurry out of harm's way.

They wouldn't make it.

"Silver, don't stop!" Sadie shouted.

I wanted to help them, but I couldn't.

Suddenly, that strange, loud screeching sound erupted all around us, and the ground stopped shaking. Trees stopped snapping, which told me the wall had stopped moving.

But we weren't safe.

The water, the debris, the mud—none of that had stopped, and it was coming straight for us.

The enormous brown wave of debris ripped through the forest, soaking the ground. People fell as the water swept through and dragged bodies along with the current. Terrified screams and shouts echoed all around me as people floated through the forest. Some landed hard against trees, their cries stopping abruptly. Others were squashed by heavy furniture, and their bodies went limp.

As the water moved closer and closer to me, I stiffened, preparing myself for the impact.

But nothing could have prepared me.

It crashed into my legs with such force that it threw me onto my back, my head splashing hard into the mud under me. The water dragged me down the forest path for what felt like minutes, and I closed my eyes every time my head fell back under water.

The taste of mud and fish slipped over my tongue. The slimy texture occasionally went right into my nose, making me cough and gag, only to swallow more water.

I felt a hand reach for me several times, but I couldn't tell who it was. And I couldn't grab it, either.

Eventually, the water thinned out, and I slid over the muddy trail until I came to a complete stop.

Moans filled the air as people slowly stood. Some rubbed their heads, their ribs, their arms, while others lay limp, unresponsive.

There was a moment of shock. People sat upright, blinking away mud from their eyes. Then, several people jumped up and started searching through the thick mud, their entire shins covered in brown goo.

"You! You okay?"

"Over here!"

"Help!"

"She's stuck! Someone help!"

Everyone scrambled to help those in need. A few people lay crushed under logs, and it took several muscular bodies to free them. Whether or not they'd survived, I wasn't sure. All I could think about was finding my friends.

"Sadie!" I called out.

"I'm here," came her voice.

I ran to her, throwing my arms around her neck. She was covered in mud from head to toe, her blue eyes looking like little sparkling gems over her brown cheeks.

"I'm okay," she breathed. "Let's find the others."

Ahead of us, James came running, his body clear of any mud. He must have driven the rover out into the field. I was thankful he'd gotten people to safety and that Krampus had done the same.

James ran a hand through his hair, watching us in disbelief.

He didn't know what to do.

"We have some injuries!" I shouted.

James pointed a finger in the air, disappeared, then came back with a red pouch in his hands. I didn't know what it was until he approached me and said, "I have a first aid kit. Who needs help?"

I didn't know where to start.

I still couldn't believe what had happened.

"A lot of people," Sadie said for me.

James nodded and made his way through the mud, looking for anyone in need of help. He pointed at people, only to receive either a quick wave—a gesture signifying they were okay—or a motion asking him to come closer.

A faint cry caught my attention.

It had come from my right, a bit off the main path.

Sadie's head snapped sideways—she'd heard it, too.

"What was that?" I asked.

"I don't know," she said. "Come on."

We ran toward the sound. It was a lament— someone in pain.

"Over here!" Sadie said.

She dropped to her knees, mud splashing onto her thighs. Pinned to the ground under a sizable two-legged table was a young boy—five or six years old.

"Help me," Sadie said, grabbing one of the legs.

I bent my knees, grabbed the table, and lifted it as hard as I could.

The boy cried out, but I couldn't tell if it was from pain or fear.

We managed to shift the heavy table over,

and Sadie rushed to the boy to pull him out of the mud. He didn't cry when she lifted him into her arms, which told me his legs were okay. The little boy wrapped his arms and legs around her and dug his face into her neck, sobbing.

"It's okay," she said, rubbing his back.

"Liam!" a woman cried. She ran so fast that she slipped in the mud several times. "Liam, oh, Liam!"

Sadie handed her the boy, who kept sobbing while saying, "Mommy!"

"Oh, thank you! Thank you!" she said to Sadie, hot tears forming white lines through the dirt on her cheeks.

It took several hours to get everyone out of the forest. Unfortunately, not everyone survived. Many cried, mourning over their loved ones' bodies. Some didn't want to leave the horrific scene. Instead, they lay next to the bodies, sobbing.

I wanted to vomit.

How did this happen?

I sat with my back against the bus's tire, simply resting. Krampus ran around, offering food and water to those who looked like they needed it most.

"Wh-what happened?" someone asked, almost unable to catch their breath.

People shook their heads.

No one knew.

"The wall..." someone said. "It came at us."

"But why?"

"How?"

"It's never moved before!"

The voices stopped the moment Ari came out of the forest, marching with her stiff arms swaying on either side of her.

Unlike everyone else, she didn't look heartbroken or afraid.

She looked angry.

Her eyes landed on me, and I swallowed hard. Would she blame me for this? I'd already told her I felt as though destruction followed me everywhere I went. Was this my fault?

The moment she approached me, I stood up. "Ari, I'm so sorry—"

"Do not apologize, Silver of Lutum," she said. "You are not to blame for such a horrible act."

While I appreciated her words, I felt partially responsible.

"I want to know who did this," she said.

Why was she asking me? I didn't know.

She must have sensed my hesitation.

"What does your gut tell you?" she asked me.

I didn't hesitate this time. "The Elites."

She jabbed the bottom of her spear into the grass, raised her chin, and blew out a long breath through her nose. "Then the Elites shall die for this."

Visit **shadeowens.com** for more works by Shade Owens, including book #5 of The Immortal Ones series.

www.ingramcontent.com/pod-product-compliance
Lightning Source LLC
Chambersburg PA
CBHW032146190726
48290CB00005BB/1430